Extorris

By
Raphael Lucchesi

ISBN-13 978-0-692-82699-7

For My Parents

After a moment, the green glow came back, but this time, it came from a tiny baby dragon that was sitting on top of the eggshells. The little dragon was beautiful. Its scales were black, with that green glow coming from them, and its belly was white. Its wings were still delicate since it was only a hatchling, but it would soon become big and strong.

He wore nothing but a torn shawl and baggy brown pants covered in patches. He looked sickly, and he had dried mud all over him. Arael felt a nasty feeling in his chest as soon as he saw him…

Only, it wasn't quite a nightmare this time; it was a memory…

CHAPTER ONE

Pneumati

Breckenridge Village was especially sunny this day. Many people frequented a small tavern that was placed in the center of the village. The tavern was named Macrae's, after the grandfather of the present owner, Macrae Keon Jr. Macrae Jr. was a pleasant man, who always greeted his guests with a smile. He looked menacing, with his big bushy mustache and his large muscular appearance, but he was one of the most admired people in Breckenridge.

Alongside Macrae, was his beloved fifteen year old son, Arael Keon, who worked with him every day to keep the tavern going. Arael had large silver eyes, blonde hair, and he even had the same smile as his father; though, he took on his mother's height, being more than two feet shorter than his titan of a father.

"Four pints fresh from the barrel!" Macrae said with a thick accent, common in the land that he was from.

Macrae slid pints of the popular beverage called Snifter White, across the wooden counter of the tavern to the waiting patrons. Snifter White was an old family recipe, which tasted like vanilla cream soda with a hint of white chocolate. Macrae's was known for its Snifter White not only in Breckenridge, but all over the land of Morthir. They even served it as an alcoholic beverage. The Keons always loved to make people happy with their drinks. Macrae's charged very little for their goods, which kept the customers coming in. The reason that they charged so little, was to keep the Pneumati away, for the richer you were, the more they came to take from you. Macrae also used this as a way to protect his son from being discovered by the creatures.

When the afternoon sun shone fiery orange, the rush of villagers decreased to the last four of the day. Macrae stood behind the counter, cleaning the smooth wooden surface with a wet rag. He stopped and wiped the sweat off of his brow after a day of hard work, before looking to the corner of the tavern, where his son slept in a wooden chair, exhausted. Macrae smiled at his son from behind his mustache, when suddenly the haunting nay of a stallion sounded from outside, catching his attention. The four patrons that were left in the tavern looked up as well, with widened eyes.

"They've come already!?" One said in alarm.

The tavern's patrons quickly leaped from their stools and dashed out the door, leaving everything behind. Macrae stared out the window of his tavern, as ghostly black horses emerged from the streets, bearing cloaked figures on their backs.

"Pneumati…" Macrae grumbled.

Macrae left his rag on the countertop, and walked to the corner of the tavern where Arael slept, before gently shaking his son's shoulder.

"Dad?" Arael said with tired eyes.

"It's time to hide son, the Pneumati are here," said Macrae. Macrae helped his son stand and took him to the back of the tavern, where there was a trap door that he had built just for Arael. He opened the trapdoor and let Arael climb inside. "Stay here until I say," he said.

"I know. I'll wait." Arael smiled, being used to this situation.

Macrae smiled back at Arael, closing the trap door and then returned to the counter, to wait for the Pneumati. Through the window, he could see the creatures taking things away from the people of Breckenridge, and piling them into a wooden cart.

"Stingy buggards…" Macrae frowned as he took a swig of alcoholic Snifter White.

The Pneumati made their way closer to the tavern, stopping at the little feed shop across the way, owned by the Crabbleton family. The creatures stood around Mrs. Crabbleton, demanding an offering as the old woman begged them for mercy. Macrae watched as two of the creatures pushed Mrs. Crabbleton out of the way and stormed into her shop. The old woman cried desperately as one of the foul creatures held her back with its sword. Macrae was curious to know what was happening, because it seemed the Pneumati were being pushier than usual... As he peered out the window he saw two of the creatures finally come out of the old woman's store, with a young girl in their grasp. Macrae's eyes widened, and his skin crawled at the sight. The old woman screamed as the Pneumati loaded her granddaughter Anita onto the back of a horse, tying her down.

Without thinking, Macrae stormed outside. "You can't take that child!" He yelled. The Pneumati seemed to stare in his direction – all he could see was expressionless voids where their faces should have been – before they all turned around and began to go on their way. "Hey!" Macrae followed the creature that possessed the terrified child and attempted to pluck her off of the horse.

Just as he reached for her, the Pneumati turned around, and made a horrible, ghostly screeching noise while slashing at Macrae with its sword, knocking him to the ground and leaving a shallow gash across his chest. The girl's grandmother ran screaming, as the creature's horse reared up and stomped, before they all rode away with the child and the villager's belongings.

"No!!! Anita! Anita!" The old woman cried, dropping to her knees.

Another villager came to Macrae's aid, helping him up off of the ground while others gathered around the sight.

"I'm sorry," Macrae said with wet eyes.

He never was able to do much against the Pneumati, and it ate away at his soul. Macrae watched as the Pneumati disappeared into the dark woods. He helped Mrs. Crabbleton off of the ground and then she hugged her husband who had just arrived, sobbing uncontrollably. What if that child was Arael? What would Macrae have done then? He wished that he could retrieve all of the children that the Pneumati had taken... Macrae went back to the tavern, knowing that there was nothing more he could do for the old woman or the child. He locked the door behind him for the night and went to the trap door to let his son out of hiding. Macrae's shirt was torn and bloody now, but he was okay. He made sure that his worried son knew that.

CHAPTER TWO
The Gift of Protection

Arael woke with the morning sunlight hitting his face, after having a dream that he couldn't quite remember, but it brought a smile to his face either way. He was lying on a hay stuffed mattress next to his father's mattress, in their small cottage that was placed behind Macrae's Tavern. The boy rolled over, taking a look at his father, who was still asleep, snoring like a rumbling thunderstorm. Arael quietly stepped out of bed and put on his clothes, careful not to wake his father. The wooden floor creaked with every step that he took, making it hard to be sneaky. It was Arael's father's birthday, and he wanted to go get him a surprise gift. Arael loved his father very much, and he had been saving up his pay from the tavern to buy something special. Arael stepped out the door and gently closed it behind him to go out into the village, unattended; something that he very rarely got to do. He was not supposed to go out on his own at all but how else was he supposed to surprise his father?

Arael walked down the dirt path of Breckenridge with a smile on his face. He was excited to finally get something for his deserving father. The villagers greeted him as he passed by, and there was a group of kids around his age, playing ball in the street.

"Arael! Where's your dad?" One of the boys asked.

"He's sleeping, I wanted to run out and pick something up before he woke," Arael answered.

"Do you want to play ball?" Another asked.

"I'm sorry, I can't. I need to hurry; he's going to wake up any minute!"

Arael waved goodbye to the children and went on his way to find a store at the edge of the village. This was the farthest that he'd ever gone by himself. When Arael arrived at his destination, he was greeted by a woman with a dirty face inside of the little shop. The woman was a blacksmith. She created beautiful swords and hammers that were often purchased by the small army of knights who attempted to protect the villages. She considered herself an artist rather than a blacksmith.

"A long way from home, don't you think?" She asked, once Arael came to the stone counter.

"Yes'm, I know. I'm here to buy something for my dad," Arael said.

"What'll it be then?" She asked. Arael pointed to a sword with a green and silver hilt that hung on the wall behind the woman. "A fine one that is," said the woman.

"My dad always wishes that he can protect the villagers, so I want to buy that sword for him so that he can," Arael smiled.

The woman wrapped up the sword, and then Arael gave her almost every penny that he had in exchange. He picked up the sword, thanked the woman politely, and quickly left to get home before his father knew that he was missing. He ran with the heavy gift in his arms, passing the kids playing ball, and the villagers who greeted him earlier. He was so happy that he could finally give his father something that he deserved; but once he got near his home, he stopped in his tracks before diving behind a barrel.

There were Pneumati standing outside of the tavern. He could see his father standing with them, trying to convince them that there was no one there but himself. The Pneumati took two barrels of Snifter White that Arael and his father had worked so hard to make, and they stole a few of the chairs and tables from the tavern. They stayed at the entrance, demanding Macrae to bring forth his child. They must've found out about Arael somehow... It was only a matter of time... The Pneumati always found out about kids that were hidden from them. Maybe it was a good thing that Arael had snuck away for a moment.

"I swear, I'm the only one here!" Macrae said.

The one Pneumati that could speak English – though it wasn't so clear – insisted that they knew about Arael, and every youngling that lived in the villages, so there was no use in hiding, but after a while of searching and arguing, the Pneumati finally gave up. They swore that the next time they would find Arael and take him from Macrae, thus, they rode off into the woods once again.

Macrae put his face in his hands in a mixture of fear and relief that the evil creatures had gone, and then went into the tavern, calling Arael's name. Arael carefully came out of hiding and gingerly walked to the tavern, afraid of what his father might say. He knew that he wasn't supposed to be out without his father, and especially when he didn't know where he was. Arael opened the front door and stood in the entrance with the wrapped up weapon in his arms.

"Arael! My boy!" Macrae ran to his son and hugged him tightly. "Why did you go!? I thought they took you! Where were you!?"

"I'm sorry, Dad," Arael said sadly. "I wanted to get this for you." Macrae let go of Arael as he held the gift out to him. "It's for your birthday."

Macrae took the gift and unwrapped it, revealing the green and silver colors that decorated the sword, but he only put it to the side and hugged his son once again.

"Don't ever do that again, not for me," Macrae let go of Arael and wiped a tear from his eye. "...This is a beautiful sword. Thank you, son," Macrae sighed, picking up the sword.

"I got it for you so you can fight the Pneumati, since you always talk about wanting to do something more to protect everyone!" Arael smiled. "But you can only use it when you absolutely have to!"

Macrae lovingly rubbed Arael's hair as he hid the sword behind the counter, and the two went on with their day like any other. Macrae was quick to forgive his son, especially when he meant well. There was no use in punishing the boy for wanting to buy a gift for him.

CHAPTER THREE
Offering

As the days went on, the Pneumati began to appear more frequently, and nobody knew why. It was becoming harder and harder for the villagers to hide their kids. The knights of Morthir were doing their best to stop the Pneumati, but they were being slaughtered. All of the villages had been ravaged, so the people were starving and had nothing left to give to the greedy creatures.

Macrae's tavern was empty, now that nobody could afford simple delicacies. Arael sat sketching pictures of the Pneumati in his journal, in a silent corner of the tavern. He was thinking about what might become of the village with all of this chaos. He was one of very few children left who hadn't been caught, which was quite lucky since the creatures said that they were going to take him next, but they never were able to; Macrae and Arael were too careful.

"Dad, what are we supposed to do?" Arael asked, keeping his attention on his journal.

His father sat at a table, reading the village paper that the messenger had brought for him. "What do you mean, son?" He asked, licking his thumb to turn the page.

"What are we going to do about the Pneumati? The village is suffering. I'm worried."

Macrae paused. "...I'm sure that everything'll be fine," he said, unconvincingly.

Arael stood up and paced around the room. "They're not going to stop! The knights aren't able to do anything about it!" He said.

"If I could become a knight, I would, son. I would put an end to this madness. But I need to be here," Macrae said.

Suddenly, someone burst through the door, which caused Macrae and Arael to stand defensively in surprise. A man in silver armor stood in the doorway, with a sword at his hip and a helmet on his head. The man was a knight, and two other knights were waiting outside on brown horses. The man walked into the tavern, approaching Macrae. The knight had a grand shield, fastened to him with a strip of leather. The shield was unlike any other that Arael had ever seen, decorated with gold, red and silver.

"Can I help you, good knight?" Macrae asked.

"Macrae Keon?" The knight asked.

"Yes sir," Macrae answered.

"I am Enzo, Sir Enzo; a knight of Mountainglaive," the knight said, out of breath.

The knight took off his metal helmet, letting his long, dark brown hair loose and revealing his face. He had a scar over his bottom lip, running down to his neck, and he had very well groomed facial hair.

"Never heard of it," Macrae said, raising an eyebrow at him.

"Yes, indeed," Enzo smiled, first setting his helmet on top of a table, and then sitting down in exhaustion. "Mountainglaive is only known to a select few."

"Are you okay?" Arael asked, gripping his journal.

Enzo smiled at Arael, looking him over. "Yes, boy, I'm fine. The Pneumati felt that I wasn't welcome here, so I had to take care of that," he said. "Now... I've come to ask a question of you both."

Macrae went behind the counter and began filling a pint of Snifter White. "Well, we're listening. Go on ahead," he urged.

Enzo stroked his mustache thoughtfully, and then spoke, "The Pneumati are planning to take every youngling from the age of twelve to nineteen that they can find in the next seven days. I don't know their sole purpose for this, but I believe that it is to get rid of the only threat that could destroy them. My job is to save the children from this fate, and to train them at Mountainglaive to protect themselves and the rest of the land's children." Enzo paused as Macrae handed him a drink. "Mountainglaive is a special place, hidden somewhere the Pneumati will never find. The location has never been disclosed outside of its own walls. If your son is to be put into my hands, I will take him to

Mountainglaive, and he will be trained to become a knight of great power. My Chancellor's hope is that through this, the Pneumati will never take another child again, and they will soon be destroyed." Enzo paused again to take a swig of Snifter White. "So my question is – Are you willing to hand your son over to Mountainglaive for his own protection and the protection of our future?" He finished.

Macrae stared between Enzo and his son, deep in thought, while Enzo waited patiently for a reply.

"Dad, you're not going to let them take me are you?" Arael asked.

Enzo finished his drink and stood up.

"I- How do I know that I can trust you?" Macrae asked the knight.

"You don't. I'm not going to force you to do anything. It's up to you Mr. Macrae. I'm a mentor at Mountainglaive, and my only concern is to protect the younglings. It's just like sending your boy away to a school. I strongly believe that you'd be leaving him in good hands," Enzo answered, almost too honestly.

Macrae looked between Arael and the knight once more. "Can I think about it?" He asked.

"Indeed. We are coming back in three days' time to transport the children of Breckenridge to Mountainglaive. You are the only undecided parent thus far. You have until then, sir," Enzo put his helmet back on and bowed to Macrae. "Thank you for your time. I will be on my way."

With that, Enzo turned around and walked out the door, riding away on his horse with the other two knights.

"Dad!?" Arael whined.

"What, son!?" Macrae asked.

"I won't leave you! We need each other!"

Macrae kneeled down and looked into Arael's big, silver eyes. "I don't want you to go either, son. But if you stay here and the Pneumati take you, then we'll never see each other again! At least if the knights take you, I know that you'll be safe."

"But Dad!"

Macrae paused before sighing, "Okay… You can stay here…"

Arael hugged his father and Macrae hugged his son back, staring at the floor, deep in thought about what he should do. The large man was, quite honestly, afraid.

CHAPTER FOUR

Unwelcome Changes

Arael ran through the dark woods, where everything appeared warped and odd. Something was chasing him, but he was having trouble running. He couldn't see what was on his tail, and he was scared and lost. He caught a glimpse of a shadow figure from the corner of his eye and whipped his head around to see it better. There was a cloaked figure standing ahead of him between two trees, but then it disappeared. Arael began to run again, going as fast as his heavy, weighed down legs could carry him. He began hearing whispering sounds buzzing around in his head like flies, causing more anxiety to flow through his body. Suddenly, he stopped, spotting a figure lying in the leaves.

"Dad!" He screamed. He couldn't see the figure well, but somehow he knew that it was his dad. Who else could it have been? Arael ran to his father and stopped above

him with tears in his eyes. His father was dead on the ground, with horrible, bloody wounds. "No!" he cried. Suddenly, something appeared behind him, and he quickly turned around. A cloaked Pneumati was stepping closer and closer to him. Arael backed up, tripping on his dead father, which sent him backwards onto the ground. The Pneumati kept moving toward him, with no intention of stopping. "Get away!" Arael yelled. The Pneumati stopped above Arael and stared at him, with red eyes appearing from the darkness behind its hood, and then it swiftly lunged toward him, causing him to scream in terror.

Arael was suddenly awoken by his father, who was shaking his shoulder. His body jerked in panic at the sudden awakening, and his shirt was drenched in sweat. The room was still dark, and it was freezing; he didn't understand why he was being woken up at this time, though it was a relief that his nightmare was no more.

"Arael! Arael, wake up!" His father said in great haste.

"Dad? What's-"

Macrae cut him off, trying to pull him out of bed, "The Pneumati are here right now! You need to get somewhere safe!"

Arael jumped out of bed and grabbed his journal out from under the pillow before following his father, but a Pneumati had quickly made its way into their home, blocking their path. The Pneumati lunged toward Arael to grab him, but Macrae had the sword in his hand – the one that Arael had given him for his birthday – and cut the Pneumati's hand clean off, causing it to screech an ungodly, earsplitting noise. The Pneumati's hand fell to the ground and turned to stinky, black mush before a new one replaced the lost one. Macrae grabbed Arael's hand and pulled him to run. "Run, Arael! Run!" He yelled.

They ran outside, where the entire village was under attack by the Pneumati. Screaming and crying echoed throughout the streets, as Arael ran behind his father with nothing but pajamas and bare feet. What was happening!? The Pneumati had never attacked like this before! One of the Pneumati was screaming down to its army, flying on the back of a terrifying Black Ghost dragon, as it set houses on fire. The creatures that rode atop black horses chased the villagers and scooped up their kids.

"Keep running!" Macrae shouted.

A Pneumati on a black horse began chasing them, getting closer and closer; there was no way that they were going to be able to outrun the horse! Macrae pushed Arael out of the way, and they both fell to the ground, just as the Pneumati tried to catch them. The Pneumati turned its horse around and faced them to charge again while they were on the ground, but then suddenly a brown horse crashed into it, knocking the Pneumati to the ground. A man in silver armor jumped off of the brown horse and stabbed the Pneumati with his sword, killing it, thus turning it to black, smelly ooze. The man in silver armor quickly approached Arael and his father, helping them up.

"Come with me! Both of you!" It was Enzo!

Macrae and Arael ran behind Enzo, to the edge of the village, where a large wooden coach, attached to four horses was waiting. There were terrified kids inside the coach, looking out the windows with fearful eyes.

"You have to decide! We take your son now, or he dies here!" Enzo said.

"Take him! Keep him safe, knight!" Macrae decided.

"Dad!" Arael cried.

Macrae grabbed Arael's shoulders. "Listen to me, Arael! You have to go! We have no choice! I'll be fine on my own, but I need you to be safe!" He explained.

"No, Dad, no! I won't leave you!" Arael sobbed.

"You have to! I'll see you again, son! Be strong! Know that I will always love you!" Macrae said, hugging Arael.

"We need to leave now!" Enzo said as one of the knights shot an arrow at an approaching Pneumati.

"Take him and go!" Macrae said, picking up his son and shoving him into the coach.

The driver of the coach immediately whipped the horses to a gallop, moving the coach down the dirt road, farther and farther away from the village.

"Dad! Dad!" Arael cried, reaching his hand out the window as he watched the black dragon blow fire at the only home he had ever known, before his father ran away, disappearing from his sight; maybe forever. Enzo ran behind the coach and jumped onto the back, slashing a pursuing Pneumati. All of the terrified kids cried inside the coach, watching as they left their homes and families behind. Arael only stared blankly at the burning village, petrified and afraid. He felt alone and he didn't know when the next time he would see his father was going to be...

CHAPTER FIVE

Castle in the Mountain

Early morning came and the sun was just peeking pink on the horizon. The coach was still traveling, with the children inside. The younger children were asleep, being comforted by the older ones. Arael sat at the back of the coach with an exhausted, blank stare, but he couldn't fall asleep after the events that had occurred just hours before. He had his journal open in his lap, with sketches of his father all over the page.

The landscape outside was peaceful and still, with trees blowing gently in the cool fall air. Arael looked out the window ahead of him, where he could see the path that they were traveling. Next to the path was a sign, which read 'Welcome to the Kingdom of Tarragon.' Arael looked up from the sign, where he could see the kingdom down the hill. The kingdom was beautiful, and it looked as though it had never been touched by the dirty hands of the Pneumati.

Before they reached the kingdom of Tarragon, they suddenly went off the path, hitting rocks and branches. The sleeping kids woke up at the sudden roughness of the ride, wondering what was going on. Arael was sure that they were heading toward the kingdom, but that didn't seem to be the case anymore. He hoped that they were almost to their destination.

"Sorry about the rough ride," Enzo said from behind the coach. "Our journey ends soon with this very path. Just watch and you'll see. You're a lucky group; you didn't have to travel nearly as far as other younglings."

The children all looked out the windows of the coach; all that they could see were trees and large jagged mountains sticking out above them. They wondered what it was that they were looking for. They kept on moving, until they were out of the woods. The edge of the woods came out to a cliff, and the path that they were on was the only way to keep moving forward. The kids leaned out of the windows to see what was below the path that had now become a land bridge. It was a straight drop down on both sides, into crystal clear water that led far away to a narrow opening between two huge, jagged rocks, where the morning sun was beautifully visible.

The land bridge kept leading up toward what looked like just another rocky mountain, until one child pointed toward it and told the others to look. As they got closer and closer to the mountain, it was becoming clear to them that part of it was actually an enormous castle. The kids stared at it in awe as they came to the front of the mountain castle, and to the end of the path, where there was an open space made of cobblestone. Many other coaches that looked the same as the one they were riding in were sitting in front of the castle, while kids stood in a crowd, waiting for the last coach to return.

"Welcome to Mountainglaive," said Enzo, before hopping off of the back of the coach.

Arael was actually able to crack a smile when he saw the enchanting castle and its beautiful scenery. The driver of the coach brought the horses around a large, circular garden and parked. Enzo opened the door of the coach and let all of the kids out to stand with the others. The kids spoke to each other in nervous confusion, unsure of what was going on. Arael pushed through the crowd, wandering around, when another boy caught his eye. The boy looked lost, standing all alone. He had nappy brown hair in an undercut ponytail, and he wore raggedy pajamas just as Arael did. Arael seemed to have caught the boy's eye as well, for he approached him as soon as he saw him.

"Hello, my name is Orias," the boy said. "Do you know what's happening?"

"I'm not sure," Arael answered.

Orias looked around, biting his lip. "I think I'm going to stay with you if that's alright. I'm nervous," he smiled.

Arael nodded yes to Orias. Just then, an older woman emerged from the grand, decorated doors of the castle and walked out to the edge of the steps with two knights by her side. The woman wore faded robes, and she had long red hair; she was quite beautiful.

"Welcome students," she said with a warm smile. "I know that you are all afraid. I couldn't even imagine what you've been through. But, this place is safe, and you will learn everything you need to know to protect yourselves. I am Chancellor Fruke Hofmeister, and I am the keeper of this castle. Here, we will teach you numerous things to ready you for what lies ahead, and I truly hope that you will all be happy here. Today, we will take you on a tour and show you a few demonstrations, and then we will let you settle in to your new home. The elder knights will be your guides and your mentors. They will take it from here. If you ever need me, I will know it simply with a thought. It is an honor to be here with you, and again, welcome to Mountainglaive."

With that, the woman suddenly disappeared into a red stream of smoke, quickly flying up to the highest point of the castle. The kids stared in astonishment, unsure of what had just happened.

"Indeed," said Enzo, with a cocky smile.

One of the knights that were standing with Fruke, stepped forward. He was a red headed man, with a bushy mustache, and he was noticeably quite tall and bulky, especially with his knight armor. "My name is Sir Gwenael. Follow me at all times, I will begin the tour. Please, come in," he said, with a funny accent.

The kids exchanged confused glances, and then began walking slowly behind Sir Gwenael, while the other knights kept them together. As soon as they walked into the castle, the kids gasped in awe. The castle was enormous, and there were beautiful decorations all over the ceilings, walls, and even the floors.

"This is the vestibule of course. It is the main gateway to any place in the castle, as you can see by the many hallways and staircases," said Sir Gwenael.

"This is the coolest place I've ever seen!" Orias said.

Arael admired the castle quietly; it looked ancient, along with all of the furniture. The hallways were very long and decorated with old paintings, armor pieces, and mirrors. They walked on a worn red carpet that led the way through one of the hallways. Arael saw shields and swords placed next to each other on the walls with knights' regalia decorating them, and the banners that went with them.

One kid spoke out from the crowd, "So, are we really to become knights like you?" She asked.

"Indeed," Sir Gwenael answered.

This echoed in the back of Arael's mind; Arael being an actual knight. Sir Arael Keon, knight of Mountainglaive. Arael liked the sound of this. It hit him: he actually wanted to become a knight, to protect others and to bring an end to the Pneumati. He'd never been away from his home, and it had never been easier to realize how miserable it actually was to be tormented by those creatures all his life. He felt as though he was home, knowing that he could do things that he could never have imagined. Arael stared at his reflection in the armor on the walls as he walked by. He was to become the greatest knight that there ever was. He had a purpose now; he wasn't going to be controlled by the Pneumati anymore, and he was going to make everyone proud.

CHAPTER SIX

Strange Faces

The knights had finished showing the group of new students around the enormous castle, and had now begun showing them a few demonstrations of what they would learn throughout their time at Mountainglaive. The knights explained that they would train the kids in many different subjects, including combat, blacksmithing, horse riding, even magic and special creatures. Enzo said that they may be able to ride real life dragons when the time came. Everyone was excited about the dragons. The knights also explained that after they taught them everything they needed to know, Chancellor Hofmeister and some people called 'Legion Masters' would decide when they believed they were ready to take a final test to become knights of Mountainglaive.

Only those who passed the test were to become knights. That was supposed to happen after the first quarter of the year. The twelve students with the highest scores in all classes would be chosen to be in something called legions, which were teams with four special types of knights, consisting of riders, helms, mages and protectors. Once they became knights with their own legions, there was no telling what kind of grand quests they would get to go on!

Arael wanted to begin so badly, so that he could become one of the kids chosen to be in the legions, but it looked like it wasn't going to be easy. In the entire castle, there were already more than a thousand children. Orias wanted to become one of the top twelve as well, so he and Arael made a deal to help each other throughout their time at Mountainglaive, to make sure that they would become the best. If one of them got into the legions and the other failed, they would be sure to choose each other as the first member of their legion.

Everyone stood inside a spacious room, with a square stage that was made for dueling. A new knight stood on top of the stage, talking about the combat class that he was the mentor for. This knight's name was Sir Cornelius, and he looked about as plain as a person could be; but he didn't believe that he was plain at all. Arael and Orias stood up against the edge of the stage, watching Sir Cornelius pace around as he explained simple fighting moves and stances. They were excited to learn these things, and eager to start as soon as possible.

"Now, I would like to demonstrate a quick match to all of you," Sir Cornelius smiled.

The mass of youngsters cheered in reply.

"But I'll need a volunteer," Sir Cornelius said, pointing toward the new students.

Orias and Arael raised their hands, along with only a few others. Not a lot of them were comfortable enough to volunteer yet. It was completely understandable, considering what they all had recently been through, arriving at a new place with strangers and all.

"You there! Why don't you come on up here, eh?" Sir Cornelius said, pointing toward one of the kids.

Arael and Orias whined in disappointment as they watched a tall boy climb up onto the stage. The boy had wavy, taupe white hair, pulled to the back of his head into a messy ponytail, while the rest of his hair hung over his face, covering his right eye. The color of his hair was strange to see on a person so young. He wore nothing but a torn shawl and baggy brown pants covered in patches. He looked sickly, and he had dried mud all over him. Arael felt a nasty feeling in his chest as soon as he saw him... The boy's bare feet tapped against the marble stage as he walked across it, and then he stopped in front of Sir Cornelius.

"Good then! Take this sword! I promise that I will do you no harm, these are not lethal blades for they are made of wood," Sir Cornelius tossed a sword to the boy. The boy caught the sword with a friendly smile and stood in a defensive position, ready to duel. "Observe!" Sir Cornelius said egocentrically. "Always salute your dueling partner!" Sir Cornelius and the boy saluted each other, bringing their wooden swords to their noses and back to their sides. "Begin!" Sir Cornelius lunged toward the boy, missing completely after the boy dodged his attack. Sir Cornelius paused for a moment, dumbfounded that he had missed as the crowd of kids chuckled at him. "I see... I believe I've made an unwise decision. Clearly, you know what you are doing. Again!" Sir Cornelius attacked the boy again, being humiliated not only a second time, but a third and fourth, causing the chuckling of the kids to become an uproar of hysterical laughter.

Arael and Orias stared at the boy in astonishment.

"How are we going to beat that guy!? He's good right off the top!" Orias said.

"I- I don't know... I hope that they're not all like that, or else we'll never get into the legions!" Arael answered, pulling his cheeks down with his hands.

Orias and Arael began to feel defeated, along with Sir Cornelius, who stared at the boy on the stage in disbelief. Sir Cornelius gave up and slid his wooden sword into a box on the side of the dueling stage.

"V- very good. You see, I let you win. This demonstration has now come to a finish," Sir Cornelius said, clapping slowly.

The boy walked toward him to hand the sword back, causing Sir Cornelius to flinch in fear. The crowd laughed even harder at this, seeing that Sir Cornelius wasn't as tough as he thought, recoiling at but a child. Sir Cornelius stood up straight and adjusted his uniform, taking the sword from the boy. The boy respectfully bowed his head to Sir Cornelius and gracefully leapt off of the stage. It looked like the boy thoroughly enjoyed the duel. The look on his face was so innocent that he probably didn't even know that he was humiliating the man.

"Right... Be off with you then. I'm sure that the dining hall is ready for you by now. If you would follow Enzo, he'll show you the way," said Sir Cornelius, waving them off like animals.

"I hope you're all hungry," Enzo said.

Enzo was already everyone's favorite knight. He was more real than all of the others; he didn't have anything to prove nor did he have anything to hide. The kids all cheered in excitement as they followed Enzo to a great room with two tables that stretched across the entire length of it. There was a round table at the very end of the dining hall, and a huge, lifelike bronze dragon that clung to the ceiling. The granite walls were adorned with portraits of what looked like historical battles, along with the armor of knights that fought in the battles. The kids smiled in excitement and followed the knights as they showed them to their seats. Orias snuck to a seat next to Arael so that he could speak to him. The kids were all so happy; they'd never seen a dining room so grand and full of history in their entire lives. They sat as they were served by short little brown cloaked creatures, who looked as though they were floating. The creatures set cider and large plates of food in front of the excited youngsters; the food smelled so delicious.

"What are they?" Orias asked.

One of the cloaked creatures stared at him with a ghostly grey face.

"They're Cocos. They're very friendly and great cooks at that," Enzo said, as he passed by.

Orias waved at the Coco that was staring at him, and then it slowly waved back before it turned around with the others and disappeared into another room. The kids dug right into their food, almost forgetting that there were any worries at all. Arael stared at the white cider that the Cocos gave him, which reminded him of the Snifter White that his dad served back at Macrae's Tavern.

"I wish my father was here. I hope that he's okay," Arael said.

Orias looked up from his food, with a mouthful of chicken leg that he had just torn into. "I miss my parents too... I'm sure your dad is fine though," he smiled.

"I hope you're right." Arael's eyes drifted around the room, looking at everyone tearing into their supper. He spotted the boy that had dueled with Sir Cornelius, sitting at the other side of the table not too far away. The boy ate slowly, staring at the plate, ignoring the noise around him. "There's that boy that fought Cornelius," Arael said, pointing him out to Orias.

"He looks lonely," Orias stated.

"He's a bit odd, I'd say."

"Why is that?" Orias chomped another chunk off of his chicken leg.

"I don't know. There's just something weird about him. He's acting different than everyone else."

"I'm sure that he's only trying to adjust to this. I know I still am," Orias shrugged, taking another big bite of food and then burping loudly.

The angry sound of yelling suddenly surfaced from the other side of the room, catching everyone's attention. Orias and Arael watched as they saw food fly up into the air, while a girl yelled out, "How dare you!"

More food flew through the air, when suddenly, a chunky boy with red hair and freckles slid across the table, skidding to a stop in front of the two. Orias plucked his plate and drink off of the table before the kid knocked it all down, continuing to casually stuff his face. Everyone stared as a rather intimidating looking girl with dark hair and violet eyes stomped across the table and stopped above the chunky boy.

"You keep your trap shut next time you come across me!" She yelled, pointing her finger at the kid, just before she finished him off by kicking him straight in the gonads.

The chunky kid rolled over, clutching his sensitives as the male kids made pained noises of fellow feeling.

"What is going on over here!?" One of the knights in the room yelled. The knight grabbed the girl, and another grabbed the chunky kid and dragged them away. "That is not how we are going to start this off!" Said the knight.

Enzo walked back into the room. "What a mess..." He said, shaking his head no. "Thus, ends suppertime! Follow me now to your quarters! Fruke has assigned you all places to sleep."

The kids grumbled in disappointment as they all stood up and followed Enzo. The room that Arael was assigned to was almost up at the very top of the castle. There were six beds inside for six boys, and each bed was made with comfortable fabric and fluffy pillows, with a chest at the side of each. Orias was assigned to this room as well, with his bed placed across from Arael's in the beautiful space. They immediately jumped on top of the beds and admired the dome shaped ceiling, painted like the night sky above them. The beds were so soft and comfortable that they just wanted to fall asleep then and there.

Enzo stood in the doorway, making sure that everyone was accounted for. "Please feel free to use the washroom, which is located all the way down the hall to the left. In the morning, we will begin your full experience here at Mountainglaive," he smiled. "Oh! There's one more bed left in here." Enzo looked into the hall for the last boy that was supposed to be in that room. "You there!" He pointed down the hall to someone that Arael couldn't see. "Come on in here, son, don't be shy." He started waving someone down. "There we are."

Arael and Orias stared curiously at the boy as he walked in. It turned out to be the same boy that they watched duel with Cornelius. The boy looked around nervously as he slowly walked straight to his bed and sat down without making any eye contact.

"Righto! Have a very good night! I'm sure that you're all tired. As am I! See you in the morning!" Enzo said, closing the door behind him as he left.

The six boys in the room looked at each other in awkward silence.

"So…" Orias said.

"I'm not really tired yet," Arael said.

"Neither am I," said another boy in the room.

Orias looked at the boy that dueled with Cornelius, and then stood up from his bed and approached him. The boy looked up at him in silence, with a sad smile on his face. He looked like he was sleep deprived.

"Hi!" Orias said. "You're cool! How did you get so good at fighting?" Orias plopped himself down on the boy's bed, right next to him.

"My father trained me, actually," the boy said happily, with no hesitation. Nobody expected him to be so quick to answer.

Arael stayed on his bed, watching Orias and the boy. Something about the boy still felt odd to him, but he didn't know what it was. Though he seemed friendly, he didn't like him, yet he was fascinated all at the same time.

"Cool! So, is your father a knight?" Orias asked.

The boy put his feet up on the bed comfortably, answering his questions, "No, he's not really a knight."

Arael noticed that the boy's right eye was clouded over like that of a blind man's eye as he pushed his light hair out of his face... And there was a strange scar over it that looked as though it was created from magic rather than a weapon.

"How did you get that cool scar? Not to be rude," asked another boy from across the room.

"Oh, not at all. Of course, it was my father... He trained me, but he was never friendly about it," said the boy.

"Oh, I'm sorry," said the boy across the room, embarrassed that he had asked such a sensitive question.

"Why? I'm not sad about it. I... love my father."

Arael and Orias stared at him in confusion. "Is your father magic?" Orias asked instantly.

"Yes. But so am I," the boy answered. "Aren't you?"

Orias looked at Arael, trying to think of an answer. "Am I?" He asked.

Arael laughed at his new friend's silliness in reply.

"I'm sure that you are. Everyone is. You just have to find it is all. I believe that this place will teach you how to find it, if I'm not mistaken," the boy explained.

"Cool!" Orias exclaimed.

"Oh! I completely forgot to introduce myself," the boy said, holding his hand out to Orias politely. "My name is Virgil Capello."

Orias accepted Virgil's hand and introduced himself in turn, "I'm Orias. Orias Megalos!"

Virgil smiled happily, when they were interrupted by one of the other boys in the room. "Do you mind? I'm trying to sleep!" He said.

Orias and Virgil looked at each other and shrugged, before Orias went back to his own bed to sleep, along with all of the other souls in the great, old castle. As the light of the candles in the room were put out, Arael stared at Virgil with watchful eyes, trying to find out why he was having such strange feelings about him. Who was this peculiar boy? Arael had to stay up for a little while longer, with the light of a single candle near his bed. He sketched pictures of the castle, and the new faces that he'd seen that day, including Virgil.

CHAPTER SEVEN

The Insignia on My Chest

"Arael! Arael!" Arael heard his name being called. He was back in Breckenridge, standing in the middle of the burning village. Pneumati were all around him, killing and capturing the villagers. He was reliving the horror of the night before.

"Arael!" He heard his name being called again.

"No!" Arael yelled, when suddenly somebody grabbed his shoulder from behind.

He quickly sat up in bed with a cold sweat, gasping for air as he realized that Orias was standing by his bedside, calling his name. Orias stared at Arael in confusion, as Virgil and the other boys turned their heads to look as well.

"Did I wake you from a bad dream?" Orias asked.

Arael wiped the sweat from his brow and answered, "Yeah... It was about my home... Don't worry about it. Why did you wake me up?"

"Look!" Orias said, pointing to a box, placed on top of the chest at the other side of Arael's bed.

There were similar boxes placed on the chests all around the room. Arael crawled out of his bed and plucked the box off of the chest to examine it.

"What's in it?" Arael asked.

"Don't know. We can't get them open," Orias answered.

Arael stuck his fingers in a crack between the lid and the box, trying to pry the top off with no luck, but then as he let go, all of the boxes in the room suddenly opened on their own. The boys all looked at each other, and then they looked in the boxes and pulled out the contents. There were black, knight uniforms inside; boots, pants, shirts, belts and surcoats, but they didn't have any knight symbols on them yet, like the ones that Enzo and Sir Cornelius displayed on their chests. There weren't even any decorations on them, they were just pure black.

Arael looked into his box once again and found a note inside, so he picked it up and read it out loud, "There's a note. It says 'Good morning students, here are your instructions for the day: Please dress in your new uniforms, and be ready by zero eight hundred hours, then come to the dining hall for some breakfast. You have been noticed by the Chancellor and will be assigned a legion master that best fits you. This will be decided during breakfast. After this, your first class will be with

Sir Dante Enzo, who will tell you where to go from there. Good day.'"

They all looked at each other – Orias, with a big grin on his face – and then they all immediately began dressing themselves in their new uniforms and cleaning up for the morning. Once they were done getting dressed, they looked at themselves in a big mirror on the wall, admiring how great they looked. Virgil looked like he'd never worn clothes in his life, petting the fabric over his stomach and admiring the loose sleeves.

Arael glanced back at his journal, before deciding to leave it where it was. Next, he opened the door of the bedroom and all of the boys followed him down a huge staircase that spiraled through all of the floors. Finally they came to the foot of the stairs where Enzo was standing near the dining hall, next to a suit of armor. All of the other students were already waiting for their breakfast, causing a loud ruckus inside the room.

"You took the stairs?" Enzo asked, like they had done something stupid.

The boys looked at each other in confusion.

"How else were we supposed to get down here?" Arael asked.

"The mirror! I'm sorry, I must've forgotten to tell you! They're relatively new, so even I don't remember to use them sometimes!" Enzo laughed. "When you walk into any mirror in the castle, it'll take you wherever you need to go. The castle is so big, that it will take forever to get from one place to another! Well... Take your seats, we're about to begin assigning you your legion masters!"

Three of the boys took off in one direction, while Arael and Orias went to the table together, leaving Virgil behind. Arael and Orias sat down as the Cocos came out and gave each student their breakfast, complete with fresh orange juice. Orias reached his hand out to one of the Cocos, trying to get it to shake hands with him, but the Coco didn't understand what this meant and only drifted away. Orias stood up from the table and followed the Coco to find out where it was going, but then he suddenly smacked his nose against the wall as the Coco passed through it.

"Ow!" Orias said, rubbing his nose.

Arael giggled at his foolishness, and then they heard trumpets sounding at the far end of the dining hall where the round table was, getting all of the students' attention. The loud room became silent with nothing but a few whispers from the kids, as they watched the Chancellor come into the room and clear her throat.

"Good morning," she said. "I'm sure you've all read your notes. So let us get started. Shall we?"

Sir Gwenael stepped forward and opened up a scroll, calling out the first child's name to be assigned a legion master, "Ego Idun, please come forth."

All of the students watched as the girl who had beaten up the chunky boy the day before, got up from the table and walked to the end of the room, stopping in front of the Chancellor. The Chancellor and the girl looked at each other for a moment, and then the Chancellor made the girl turn around to face the others.

"Ego Idun, you have been assigned to the legion master, Scorpios," she said.

Chancellor Hofmeister tapped Ego's head with her finger, which caused her uniform to suddenly begin changing. Violet outlines faded onto her clothing, and a symbol of a scorpion appeared on her chest. The children gasped in awe and cheered, as Ego looked at her uniform.

"How'd she do that!?" Arael asked.

Ego bowed her head to the Chancellor and then walked back to her seat, as Sir Gwenael began calling up student after student; Fromm Flink to Virgionas, with the color grey decorating her uniform and a picture of an angel on her chest. Alle Sterben to Librona, with the color orange decorating his uniform, and a picture of iron scales on his chest. One after another, the students were decorated with their legion masters' regalia; it was fascinating and exciting to everyone.

"I wonder how they know our names," Orias said.

"I don't know. Maybe it's magic," Arael answered.

"Orias Megalos," Sir Gwenael called.

"Good luck," Arael said to Orias before he got up and approached the Chancellor.

The Chancellor smiled at him and then turned him around, tapping his head as he smiled in excitement.

"Orias Megalos, you have been assigned to legion master, Sagia."

Orias watched as his uniform began to decorate itself with royal blue, and then a bow wielding centaur appeared on his chest. "So cool!" He said, bowing his head to the Chancellor and then hopping back to Arael excitedly.

Arael and Orias admired his newly decorated uniform, touching the colors in amazement. He looked like a knight! A real knight! Arael couldn't wait for his own name to be called, so that he could look like a real knight too! He was almost jealous that Orias was called before him; he didn't have to wait too long until his name was eventually called though.

"Arael Keon, come forth!" Sir Gwenael announced.

Arael smiled and jumped up from his seat, quickly approaching the Chancellor. He did the same as all of the others, turning around to face the crowd. He felt Fruke's finger touch the top of his head, and then he felt a slight tingle go through his body.

"Arael Keon, you have been assigned to legion master, Ariese," she said.

Arael watched his uniform change. Red decorations covered the black fabric, and then the insignia appeared on his chest; his symbol was the head of a ram, with curly horns. Finally, he was one step closer to being a knight. His father crossed his mind, and he became sad. He had to do this for his father. He would become strong for him in exchange for all of the years that he had protected him. Now he was going to be able to protect his father, and everyone else from the evil Pneumati.

Areal began walking back to his seat as Virgil's name was called. He passed the boy as he came for his turn. Arael looked at Virgil, seeing his smiling face, but a sudden burst of anxiety hit him, which seemed to have come straight from the boy. Arael stopped and turned around, staring at him as he walked up to the Chancellor. Arael's heart was pounding in his chest. Everything seemed to have slowed down as he felt dread coursing through his veins.

"Arael!" Orias called.

Arael looked over his shoulder at Orias, who was waving at him, excited to see his new decorations. He looked back at Virgil as his uniform was being decorated with gold, and the symbol of a lion, belonging to Leodegrance. He looked into Virgil's dead eye and narrowed his eyes at him, knowing that this feeling was something that was coming from the boy, it wasn't just Arael.

As Virgil stepped away from the Chancellor, Arael lost the abnormal feeling that he had gotten from him, causing him to snap out of the sort of trance that he was in. Arael looked around and watched Virgil sit back down, so he did the same, going back to Orias, but he still couldn't stop staring at Virgil, trying to figure out what was happening. Every time he went by, he sent Arael a freaky feeling, and Arael didn't like it.

CHAPTER EIGHT
Charmed and Vexed

Arael and Orias stood next to each other in a vast field, just outside of the great castle. It was the only field in the rocky terrain. It was quite beautiful, like an oasis protected by natural barriers. An island of trees was nearby, sharing the same land as the field. The sound of ocean waves crashed in the distance.

The children had been separated into groups, since there were so many of them in Mountainglaive. Orias and Arael happened to have been in the same group, after Enzo decided that he didn't want to separate them, because they had already become good friends. Their group of students stood in two lines across from each other as Enzo paced in front of them with his hands behind his back. Enzo wasn't dressed in his armor anymore, wearing loose fitting clothing like the kids were.

"Good day!" Enzo said. "Are you all ready to train with the best field training mentor in the land?" Half of the students cheered while the others stayed quiet. "Good! This class really isn't that much work until you become serious knights... But! It does tie into most of your other classes, which is why it is so important. I will teach you a little of everything throughout the days, and you'll catch on as time progresses," Enzo explained.

Enzo walked to the end of the lines of students, and gestured for them to follow him to the woods near the large field. The kids broke the neat lines that they were in before, and stopped at the edge of the woods, where a strange arch stood.

Enzo pointed toward the arch. "This is your first test, to see what you already know, so I can keep track of what you learn. I want you all to go inside the arch, two at a time. Whoever you're standing across from will be your partner," he said. Arael and Orias looked at each other in a bit of a panic; they didn't want to pair up with someone that they had never spoken to. "Now, line up again! Quickly!" Enzo demanded.

The students quickly lined up while Arael and Orias tried to stand across from each other, but when the chaos of the lines stopped, they noticed that they had made a mistake. Orias was one person too far from Arael. The person who stood in front of Arael was Virgil, and Orias was standing in front of Ego Idun.

"Aw man! Look what you did!" Ego yelled at Orias. "Now how am I supposed to pass!?" She crossed her arms in anger.

"I was trying to pair up with him!" Orias pointed to Arael. "Virgil, switch!" He said, pulling at Virgil's sleeve.

"It's too late now!" Enzo interrupted, walking between all of them. "Now! You'll have to answer some questions to move throughout the test, you will open the wrong paths with the wrong answers and the right paths with the right answers. Simple as that! You'll still be able to get out if you get too many wrong. I don't want anyone stuck in there for an eternity," he explained. "Any questions?"

The kids couldn't think of any questions to ask of him, staring at the arch. Arael looked around at everyone, and then decided to raise his hand into the air to get Enzo's attention. "Sir Enzo, why couldn't we just walk through the woods?" He asked. "I can't see any paths that you're speaking of."

"It's a magic arch. You can't cheat it; the arch is the only doorway to get into the test," Enzo explained, walking around the arch, rather than through it. "You'll see soon enough. All of this is not as it seems."

"Wow!" Orias said, still confused.

"Righto! Let's begin! Go on in, two at a time!" Enzo waved the students through the arch.

Two by two, they walked in. Arael watched them go through, wondering how they were not going to just be able to cheat off of each other. He could still see all of the other students inside... He and Virgil approached the arch and walked in together, but suddenly, Arael couldn't see the others like he thought anymore, and it was very quiet. He looked around to see that they were now in a hedge garden, with purple flowers decorating the green. The sky was blue above him and birds chirped while the sun warmed his skin. This wasn't right. It was the middle of fall! And hadn't he just stepped into the woods? Arael looked over his shoulder, where the arch was no more, only a hedge stood behind him.

"Arael? Are you ready?" He heard Virgil ask.

Arael looked to his side, where Virgil stood; he had almost forgotten about him... He looked around once more and then nodded yes to Virgil, tongue tied when it came to talking to him. It seemed as though his brain couldn't think of words to say to the peculiar boy, even if it was just a simple yes or no answer. Arael followed Virgil around a corner, where they came upon the first question engraved into a beautiful stone wall.

Virgil read it out loud, "In a four man legion of knights, the helm, the rider, the mage and the protector; which knight is the most important?"

Without pausing for a second opinion, Arael attempted to answer the question, "The helm!"

Virgil glanced at him in disapproval as the wall of stone made an unsettling chime noise and split into two, opening only the right half of the stone. They proceeded through the opening and walked to their next question.

"The answer was all of them. It was a trick question," Virgil said.

Arael looked at him with burning red cheeks, feeling like an idiot. He thought that he knew! Trick questions were unfair! He crossed his arms and looked away from Virgil as they stopped in front of the next question.

Virgil read the words on this wall out loud as well, "When faced with the power of dark magic, what is the most important spell to know?"

"How is anyone supposed to know that?" Arael asked in a bratty tone.

"Aegis," Virgil said simply, which caused the wall to make a pleasant chime this time, opening the left side for them.

Virgil walked through as Arael stayed where he was, staring at him in disbelief. Virgil was stressing him out, causing him to make an idiot of himself! Arael ran to catch up and passed Virgil to get to the next question before him.

"Not a bird, nor griffin, what whistling, feathery creature could kill you before you even knew you were bitten, producing venom that could make the darkest of souls cower?" Arael read. "Ha! Common knowledge!"

"The Shrikey snake!" Virgil and Arael answered at the same time.

The wall chimed happily as the left side opened, Arael glanced at Virgil angrily while Virgil only smiled at him. What a freak! Arael thought. They walked to the next question and the next, Virgil getting all of them right. Arael only knew a handful of the right answers, which irritated him further. Finally, they came to the last question; at least, it looked like the last one, since the wall was decorated differently than all of the others.

Arael read this one, "What is the name of the king of darkness, who rules the army of Pneumati."

Arael opened his mouth to answer, but Virgil was too quick. "Ocharos!" He answered.

The wall made a noise of disapproval and opened up on the right side. Arael laughed and pointed at Virgil, excited that he finally got a question wrong, and it was such an easy question to answer!

"How could you have gotten that wrong!? Everyone knows that his name is Dieudonne!" Arael said with a huge smile on his face. Now he was the smart guy.

Virgil looked between Arael and the wall in surprise, trying to comprehend what had just happened.

"No! That's not right! His name is Ocharos, I know that for a fact!" Virgil said in disbelief.

"Nope, you're wrong! Just accept defeat!" Arael said.

"...Forget it..." Virgil's frown suddenly turned to a soft smile as he calmed down. "Good job," he said.

"'Good job?' That's all you're going to say?" Arael asked rudely.

They walked through the opening and disappeared from the maze of hedges, coming back out into the field behind Mountainglaive. Arael looked over his shoulder, seeing the arch that they had just passed through, with no maze to be seen. Arael wondered how they could've been inside an entirely different place. He looked through the arch closely, spotting the other kids standing in pairs as if there were walls in front of them, answering the questions that Arael and Virgil had just answered.

The arch must've caused them to hallucinate the entire thing somehow.

Arael looked around again. There was a good amount of other students waiting in the field, who had already finished the maze of questions, but Orias wasn't back yet.

"So! How'd it go?" Enzo asked from behind Arael, startling him.

Arael turned around to face him. "We got most of the questions right. What an odd experience to walk through that arch though," he answered.

"The answer to the last question isn't right," Virgil added.

"Oh? Is that the one about Dieudonne?" Enzo asked, stroking his goatee.

"Yes. That's not his name."

"Dieudonne is the name that the people gave him years ago."

"Nobody knows the name Ocharos?"

"Nope. Sorry, son," Enzo shrugged.

"I guess I have to rethink solutions in this place," Virgil said to himself. "I'm sorry... Everyone has always learned differently where I'm from."

Arael saw Orias and Ego come through the arch, so he broke away from Virgil to approach them. Ego stomped away from Orias angrily, pushing passed Arael with her fists to her sides.

"How'd you do?" Arael asked.

"Not so good. It's hard to think when she's yelling at me..." Orias said in embarrassment. "How about you?"

"We did good. Virgil answered most of the questions though. So I don't know how that will reflect on me," Arael answered.

"That guy is cool," Orias said, looking at Virgil.

"I don't like him," Arael said.

"Why? Is he mean? I thought he was pretty nice!"

"He's just a freak. He gives off weird energy and I don't like it," Arael frowned at Virgil.

Virgil looked at them and smiled, waving to Orias while Orias waved back, but once Virgil made eye contact with Arael, he saw that he was not happy with him. Virgil's smile faded away and his waving hand dropped to his side. Arael only frowned at him harder, causing Virgil to turn around and go away.

"While we're waiting for the rest of the students, feel free to do as you like, just as long as you stay within my sight," Enzo shouted to the waiting kids.

Arael and Orias looked at each other, and then started walking across the field together to forget about Virgil and Ego. They talked about the quiz maze, while their feet crunched in the dead grass with every step. It was peaceful out in the field, and they were able to explore some of the obstacle courses that they would later have to complete.

Orias scanned the area and suddenly felt inclined to wander toward a small, stone building that he had spotted.

"What's that?" Orias asked, pointing toward the building.

"I don't know. I don't think we're supposed to go in there though," Arael said.

Orias walked toward the building even though Arael said that they shouldn't. They were far away from the others now, and they couldn't even see the big arch anymore. They both came to the stone building, and stared at it. It looked timeworn, and it was almost eerie, the door was old and rotten, and moss grew all over it.

"We should go in," Orias said.

Before Arael could object, Orias grabbed the door handle and yanked on it. He felt like he was supposed to go in, like there was something calling him. The door didn't budge, so Orias began pulling on it harder; Arael watched, but he hesitantly decided to help anyway. They pulled on the door together, causing it to move slightly; it was heavy for a rotten old door. They tried once more, sliding it open just enough for them to fit inside. When they looked through the new opening, they could see that it was very dark, and there were no windows to let in light; the only bit of light there was, came from the open door.

"Creepy," Arael said.

"It's cool! Let's go in!" Orias said.

Orias took a step inside, squeezing passed the door while Arael followed him. It was dusty in there, making the light from the door look thick, and there was no floor, leaving only dirt to walk on top of. Arael stopped in the middle of the room, while Orias slowly continued through. Suddenly there was a pulsing green light that he could see through the darkness. The light must've been the thing that he was drawn to, because he felt more and more enticed by it the closer he got.

"What do you see, Orias?" Arael asked.

Orias didn't answer, too fixated, as he stepped closer and saw that the light seemed to have been coming from the inside of something. He reached out and touched it, causing the light to glow even brighter. It was clear now that the light was coming from inside a great egg. He could see the silhouette of something inside the egg, and it was moving. The egg was warm to the touch and it made Orias feel happy, like it was his to keep and take care of.

"What are you doing!?" They heard. They turned around and saw Ego standing at the doorway; she was too beefy to actually get through the opening. "Are you two idiots!?" She yelled. "…Well, I know that you are, after the quiz." She pointed to Orias.

"Hey!" Orias said.

"Leave us alone!" Arael said. "You're out here too. It's not like you didn't wander off."

"I was curious. I found an egg," Orias said, keeping his hands on the egg; he was thinking about taking it.

Suddenly, Virgil showed up and pushed Ego aside. "It's okay! See, they were just curious," he said. "You two should get out of there though, you really shouldn't be here. None of us should."

"Quit acting like you know us. Why can't you just mind your own business!?" Arael snapped.

Virgil didn't answer, but instead came into the stone building with them to look around. He raised his hand into the air and snapped his fingers. "Illustro," he said, causing a small ball of white light to illuminate in the air above his hand. Virgil's light lit up the whole room, revealing what was lingering in the dark. There were stone platforms all around the room, and more huge eggs sitting on top of them. Some of the eggs were broken and others looked rotten; only a few of them still looked fine. Virgil gasped and immediately put the light out when he saw the eggs. "Those are dragon eggs, Orias! ...We need to close the door or they'll die! They don't like light."

Orias let go of the egg and then the green glow stopped. He looked between Arael and Virgil, unsure of what he was supposed to do. Orias had a hard time making decisions, and often looked to others to make them for him, but couldn't decide who to listen to.

"What makes you such an expert on everything!? What the hell are you, with those weird powers?" Arael asked.

"I'm a mage, Arael. They're not uncommon, especially here," Virgil answered bluntly. "I have experience... My father has housed dragons for many years, and also expects me to know everything, which I really don't."

"Enough excuses!"

"Why don't you just quit arguing with him and listen, Arael!? Idiots!" Ego said.

Arael threw his hands up into the air. "Fine, fine! But when we leave, I don't want to see you two anywhere near us!" He said angrily. "Come on, Orias."

Orias looked up at Arael after trying to shove the dragon egg under his shirt to steal it, but failed at this task. He gave the egg a loving pat before exiting the stone building with Virgil and Arael. Virgil closed the door behind them with some kind of magic force, so that no light would get in. As soon as they started going back to their class though, they saw Enzo running toward them.

"What are you four doing all the way out here!?" Enzo asked in alarm.

"We, we were just-" Orias started.

"Virgil and I were trying to stop them from killing the dragons or being eaten by them!" Ego said.

"Dragons? How could you possibly know that there are dragons in there?" Enzo asked, placing his fists on his hips.

Orias stepped forward, looking at the ground. "It was my fault, sir. I wanted to go in... There was a green light, so I followed it. I'm sorry..." He said.

Enzo shook his head and smiled. "It's okay, boy, but I'm sure that the Chancellor will want to speak with you all."

The teens all looked at each other and then nodded at Enzo, following him back to their class.

CHAPTER NINE
The Sharpest Sword

Arael, Orias, Ego and Virgil all sat in chairs, side by side, waiting to be punished. They were in Chancellor Hofmeister's chamber after they were caught at the stone building with the dragon eggs. The chamber was huge and quite beautifully decorated, and it was set at the highest point of the castle, so they could see the land all around them. Arael had his journal with him, sketching a picture of the dragon eggs and the small, stone building. Sketching was something that he normally did when he was nervous. Virgil looked nervous too, way more than anybody else. It was almost annoying.

They heard the sound of shoes tapping down a spiral staircase in the middle of the room. They didn't know where the rest of the staircase led to, since they were already at the highest point of the castle, but it must've led somewhere. Chancellor Hofmeister came to the bottom of the staircase and walked toward them, with her beautiful red hair flowing behind her head like silk. She stopped with her hands folded in front of herself and smiled at the teens.

"So. Curious, are we?" She asked.

The teens looked away in silence.

"I'm sorry, Miss, it was my fault. I wanted to go in there, and I wanted to take the egg," Orias said, looking at the floor.

"Don't worry, none of you are in any trouble," said the Chancellor, "I'm only glad that none of you were injured. And of course, the dragons are just fine."

They all looked up at her in confusion as to why they were in her chamber, if they weren't in any trouble.

"I see great potential in you all," the Chancellor smiled.

"Don't you see potential in everyone here?" Orias asked.

"Yes, but..." The Chancellor's words drifted off into thought. The teens waited silently for her to finish, but she never did and only walked across the room like a ghost floating about. "You may head to your next classes," she said simply.

The four teens looked at each other in confusion and then slowly stood up and walked through a tall mirror, leaving the chamber. Ego stepped through her destination's mirror first, where there were students waiting for a new class to start. She stomped away angrily and disappeared into the crowd, forgetting about the three boys. Virgil popped out of the mirror next and stopped to look around, but then Arael came out and roughly pushed him aside.

"Stupid Virgil, get out of the way," Arael said rudely, storming off to wait for class, just as Ego had done.

He didn't even stop to wait for Orias who then came out of the mirror, and had to run to catch up. They didn't say a word to each other as they joined the group that was waiting for the mentor to start class. This class was blacksmithing; there were all kinds of tools and anvils inside the dark room, and exotic swords that were decorating the walls; the mentor must've made them himself.

"Calm down, Arael. We didn't get in trouble, there's no reason to be angry," Orias said.

Arael sighed and lightened up a bit, putting his journal away as the mentor entered the room. The mentor of this class was Sir Gwenael, and he was wearing a thick apron, and leather gloves instead of the armor that he always had on.

"Good afternoon, I am Sir Gwenael, your blacksmithing mentor. Today, we're going to start off by discovering the special weapons you are destined to wield. Because what's a knight without a proper weapon after all? Next, you are going to craft your own weapons, based off of the ones that you've chosen," he said.

Everyone stayed silent, thinking about the kinds of weapons they would get to craft. They watched as Cocos came into the room, pushing carts with wooden wheels. The wooden carts carried many different weapons on them that the students could choose from. The last Coco that floated into the room brought the materials that they would build their weapons from. The Cocos parked the carts near the walls and then quietly floated out of the room, like they always did.

"Let us start, shall we? Come pick the weapon that you like. But the first one that you grab will be the one that you make, because the first choice is always the one that you are drawn to, which means it will be your best fit," Gwenael said. "One at a time. It doesn't matter if you're down to the last weapon, your weapon chooses you. This is part of finding out who you are as knights."

The students walked to the carts, and began plucking the weapons off of them. Arael wanted one of the swords, there was no other weapon that he would even begin to consider. He watched as the kids removed the swords one by one.

"Come on, come on!" Arael said to himself.

Finally Arael got to the carts; he looked around quickly, finding no swords as he paced back and forth, frantically searching. He was disappointed, unable to find anything that felt right to him. Just as he was going to give up, he spotted a beautiful sword with a silver ring at the end of the hilt that was leaning up against one of the last carts; left unseen by the others, like it was hiding there just for him to find. He picked it up and held it in his hand with excitement. This was his sword. This was the sword that he was going to make! He walked out of the way and examined the sword while Orias chose his weapon and then came to him with it in his hands. Orias had a battle axe. It fit him well, but it looked a little heavy.

"Now then. Everybody has a weapon. Go pick a station, three at each table. Once you have a station, keep your weapon with you for reference," said Sir Gwenael. "I will be helping you every step of the way, but know that you won't be making anything perfect the first time around. It's okay to make mistakes, that's why we're learning."

Orias and Arael went to the same station – which was just a stone table – and set their weapons down on top of it. A girl came to their table, who had chosen a bow and arrows.

Sir Gwenael began teaching them about safety when it came to making their new weapons. He also had them choose their materials; telling them what was best and what was worst to craft each weapon with. Those who had chosen weapons that required woodwork, were sent outside to find tree branches with the weapons and armory mentor, Lady Ida; a tall, brawny woman, that was also quite lovely in a peculiar way. Arael saw that Virgil went outside with this group; he had chosen an odd weapon that was called a swallow wand. The swallow wand was a type of staff that was usually made from a long branch with a crystal in the end, and a knife in the bottom for combat, those weapons were especially for powerful mages. An odd weapon to fit an odd person...

The students were to make many versions – drafts, of their weapons, so they could get better and better each time. Sir Gwenael didn't expect them to be good at making weapons right away, but the kids who did well the first time around would be separated to another class.

The ones who did well the first time had a better chance of getting into the legions.

CHAPTER TEN

Getting Somewhere

After nine days of hard work, Arael had finally finished making his first sword. He'd spent extra time on it, to get it in the best condition that he could. His blacksmithing skills were surprisingly good, so he was moved to the next level. He was so proud of it, but he wished that his dad could see it, so that he could be proud with him. Someday he'd get to show it to him.

The teens were in the combat class with Sir Cornelius, testing out their new weapons on hay stuffed dummies. Orias and Arael watched in terror as Ego swung her giant sword and destroyed her targets, with two mighty blows; that girl was stronger than any man that they had ever seen. It was unbelievable! Her sword wasn't just any sword, she had made a huge one that looked like a giant meat cleaver that could slice anyone clean in half. Ego named the thing Easther, and she insisted on calling it a she. Even Sir Cornelius was cowering, which really wasn't much of a surprise, since he would cower at just about anything. Ego rested Easther on her shoulder, after demolishing the dummies, and then smiled menacingly as she turned around to face the other students.

"Good, very good," said Sir Cornelius, as he clapped questioningly.

Ego went back to the others as they cleared a path for her, afraid of getting hit with the sword.

"You see. She had power behind her swing, that's the key to any successful blow, to outmuscle your opponent. Another, more deadly key is to outthink your opponent, like mister Capello over here." Sir Cornelius pointed to Virgil, who was standing on the opposite side of the group from Arael. "But, we won't be outthinking dummies! Since they don't even have a brain to be outthought! Now, who's next?"

Arael stepped forward, with his sword at his hip. "I will, Sir," he offered, excited to use his new weapon on something other than thin air.

"Good man! Remember the stance?" Said Cornelius.

Arael nodded yes and then stood in a defensive position with his sword out in front of him, while Sir Cornelius moved three dummies into position. Once Sir Cornelius got out of the way, he told Arael that it was okay to start. Arael smiled and then looked to the dummies, remembering some of the moves that he'd already been taught in practices. He quickly went for the dummy closest to him, stabbing the sword straight through its chest. The next dummy that he went for got its head sliced off, and for the last one, he ran behind it and slashed its back, spilling its straw guts all over the floor. When he was done, he placed his sword into its scabbard at his hip, and then looked to Sir Cornelius. Cornelius nodded at him and clapped, along with the others.

"Very good, Mister Keon. You handle your sword quite professionally," said Cornelius. "I'm impressed."

Arael smiled in excitement and then went back to the group where Orias was waiting. Orias didn't build his weapon well at all, so he had to use the one that was pre-made for the time being. Orias really wasn't very skilled at anything; it made Arael feel a little bad for him. Arael, on the other hand was good at a lot of things that Mountainglaive tossed his way; but Virgil was always better... Virgil was taking in the legion points like they were free candy, it was infuriating to Arael and Orias both. Legion points were what they used as grades; it was the same as percentage, but it was a lot harder to get up near the hundreds. Thirty to forty points was considered average, and eighties to one hundred was highly professional. Virgil's average points were up in the high sixties, Arael's were in the low fifties and Orias's were hanging just around thirty.

Sir Cornelius cleaned up the spilled hay and then stood before all of the students, counting them with his eyes. "I'm afraid the rest of you will have to wait until next time," he said. "On another note, I have an announcement from the Chancellor." The students looked at him, half of them eager and the other half afraid. "There are now clues and treasures hidden all around the castle. It's a bit of an extra credit exercise, but it is also a test to see how well you can use your problem solving skills. You may choose to participate or not. Once you find each treasure, you are to bring them to the Chancellor's chamber, with whomever you found it with accompanying you. This challenge may increase your chances of making it into the legions," Sir Cornelius explained. Orias and Arael looked at each other in excitement. They could do this! Following clues was easy! "I have the first clue right here." Cornelius pointed to an image of a standard knight sword that covered the surface of the dueling stage.

This image showed up in numerous places in the castle, but each one was a little bit different. The kids stared at the image, trying to figure out what it meant, while Sir Cornelius turned to leave.

"Good luck," Cornelius said.

The students all got up onto the dueling stage to take a look at the image. Most of them were confused, while others were trying to come up with ideas for what exactly it had to do with anything. Arael pulled his journal out of a pocket in his surcoat, and quickly sketched the image onto paper.

"Why do they have to make everything so hard…?" Orias whined.

"Because, Orias… Because…" Arael replied. "Follow me."

Arael was sure that he knew where this would lead. He took Orias through the mirror in the room and came out into the vestibule. There were a few other students walking around, minding their own business. Everyone had quickly learned how to navigate the huge castle pretty well at this point, but there were still a lot of areas that were left unexplored by the students. They had two days for a break now, so everyone was relieved to do what they wanted, but they had to stay within the boundaries of Mountainglaive.

Arael walked into the great hall, where the many suits of armor and shields were placed – the ones that he'd seen when they first arrived at the castle. He stopped in front of a blue shield with an image of a similar sword on it.

"It has to be this!" Arael said, pointing to the shield.

Orias examined the shield for a moment and then shook his head no. "No, the designs on the hilt aren't the same," he pointed out.

Arael looked more closely at the hilt of the image, and then looked at the one that he had sketched. "What do you mean it's not the same!?" He asked.

Orias pointed at the designs and followed them with his finger. "The designs on this shield are square-ish, but on the dueling stage design they are more like diamonds."

"Square-ish? Do you even know what you're talking about?" Arael asked in annoyance.

"Yes!" Orias said. "Why don't you ever believe me!?"

Arael didn't want to answer that question. Orias wasn't the brightest star in the sky... He wanted to quit being partners with him all the time, but he felt like it would be rude to pick somebody else. He didn't really know anybody else anyway. Orias was nice to him, so he really didn't deserve to be left out all the time. What one or both of them really needed to do, was go 'help' Mister Virgil Smarty Britches and get some extra credit for things, but that was never going to happen.

"Fine... What do you suggest we do then?" Arael asked, crossing his arms.

"There's a banner in Sir Gwenael's classroom! I think it looks more like the one on the dueling stage and your drawing!" Orias said, excitedly grabbing Arael's hand and dragging him back to the traveling mirror, which took them into Sir Gwenael's classroom. There was nobody around except for a Coco, who was cleaning up after the last class. "Hi, Coco!" Orias said, waving to the creature.

The Coco waved back, with a slow, stiff hand. It probably didn't even know what it was doing. Orias had made friends with those things. It was quite strange that he always made friends with just about anything. An egg, the Cocos, a frog that he found in his shoe a few days before; even a leech that came from a... peculiar... place in the washroom, after they walked through a pond in the woods behind the castle.

Orias took Arael to a large banner on the wall that had a knight sword decoration on it. Like he had said, the diamond designs covered the hilt of the sword. It made a little more sense to Arael now, but he still wasn't convinced yet.

"What would the next clue be then? Or where would it be...?" Arael asked.

Orias and Arael started looking around, uncertain of what they were supposed to find. Arael looked at the walls, while Orias tried the floor.

Orias suddenly leaped into the air and pointed at the banner. "Oh! Behind it! We should look behind it!" He said.

Arael nodded and then moved the banner so they could see the wall behind it, revealing a large hole where a brick was missing. Their hearts dropped when there was nothing inside the hole... It looked so off though, like something had already been taken from that place. Orias pressed the bricks around it to see if there were any secret buttons, but they still had no luck. After a while of searching, they finally gave up on the banner.

"I just don't get it..." Orias said sadly.

Arael looked at him. "Let's keep looking. We should go back and take another look at the dueling stage and that shield," he said.

"Okay..." Orias said, following Arael.

Hours and hours passed by, and they weren't able to find what they were looking for. They had gained knowledge of other clues that were separate from the one they'd been made aware of, but they just had no luck. Every time they thought they'd figured something out, they hit another dead end. When the clock struck midnight, they finally decided to give up for the day. All of the kids were excited about the clues. Some of them stayed up even later than Arael and Orias did. The two retreated to the boy's wash room, where there were many others getting ready for bed. They were all talking about the clues and it sounded to them like nobody else really found anything either...

"At least we're not the only ones," Arael said, going to one of the showers.

"Yeah," Orias said. "I wonder if anybody found anything at all!"

Orias and Arael got into the showers next to each other, where the walls in between them were as high as their shoulders. The showers were actually quite nice. There were metal chains that they had to pull to open up the water flow. The water came from an underground hot spring that enabled the students to change the temperature of the water, depending on which chain was pulled and how far.

Orias turned to the boy in the next shower over. "Schlimm, do you know if anybody found any new clues?" He asked.

Everyone called this boy Schlimm, because it was a lot more fun and easier to say than his first name – Fikri; he was one of the older students in the castle.

"No..." Schlimm answered. "Nobody did. At least that I know of."

"Wow, I thought for sure at least somebody would've found something," Orias said.

Orias quickly finished showering, doing not much to clean himself up except for a bit of rinsing. He shut the water off and went to get his pajamas on for the night. Arael stood under the water, having a moment to himself to close his eyes and think. He really did miss his father. He'd never been away from him. He hoped that he was okay... Being in a new environment with new people like this was making Arael more unfriendly toward people than he normally would be. He was always uncomfortable taking showers like this too. He wasn't used to people seeing him; it made him want to go back to the seclusion of his own washroom, even though it wasn't nearly as nice as this one.

Arael ran his fingers through his wet hair and sighed, before resting his forehead on the wall in front of him, letting the hot water hit his back. Not even a second after he touched his head to the wall, he got an unexpected vision in his head. He saw the Pneumati again, someone was screaming; struggling. "Arael! Please- help me- you have to trust me!" He heard... It wasn't a voice that he was very familiar with, but he knew that he'd heard it somewhere before, he just wasn't sure where. Next, he saw a completely different scene before blood splashed on the floor... And then that was it...

Arael opened his eyes and stared at the floor. He wasn't quite sure what to make of that vision. It felt so real and he felt terrible for whoever was calling for him, like they had been hurt for a long time. What was even more distressing was that this was his first waking vision. Every night he'd get dreams about the Pneumati doing unspeakable things... It seemed like it was getting worse and more and more frequent, but he never expected his mind to haunt him away from the bed. He hoped that this wouldn't affect his everyday life; he hoped that it wasn't the beginning of some sort of brain problem too. Now he felt paranoid.

Arael felt inclined to glance at the washroom door, and caught sight of Virgil just as he had entered. Arael watched him closely until he disappeared behind the wall in front of him. Arael shook his head and grumbled in annoyance, finally turning the water off and getting out of the shower, quickly throwing on his pajamas afterward.

Arael went around the corner when he was dressed, to go brush his teeth. He was quite serious about hygiene, he didn't want to have brown teeth... Nobody looked good with brown teeth. There weren't many boys in the washroom anymore, and Orias must've already gone to bed. It was late, so everybody was tired from looking for those clues. The washroom really was quite huge. It was bigger than Macrae's Tavern. The sounds of the last few boys taking showers echoed through the room, which was strangely comforting; but it was also a bit eerie when it bounced off of the walls, making the sounds of ghostly conversations. Steam covered the enormous mirror that hung in front of the basins, and the light above was dim. The entire castle was only lit by candles at night and sunlight in the daytime.

As Arael was brushing his teeth, Virgil came to the next basin over. Arael wished that he would've picked any basin other than the one right next to him. Arael looked at him briefly as Virgil was looking down at the drain quietly, while holding onto the sides of the basin. It was odd, but Virgil was always doing something odd... Arael looked back at his own basin and finished brushing his teeth. He heard Virgil whispering something to himself with a quiver to his voice. That was even stranger, because Virgil always showed the same emotion no matter what the situation was, and he was always calm. Arael looked up at him again and stared for a moment. It didn't look like Virgil even knew that he was there.

Arael rolled his eyes and decided to be nice to him; he didn't want to, but he knew how to put his feelings aside when somebody needed help. "Are you alright, Virgil?" He asked.

Virgil quickly looked over at him with wide eyes, obviously surprised. His mood softened to what it normally was and he smiled at Arael, wiping his eye with the back of his hand and keeping his other hand over his cheekbone. Was he crying?

"I'm fine, thank you Arael," he said. Virgil blinked, trying to hold something back, and then he stopped smiling and looked at the floor. "Have a good night," he said, quickly walking out of the washroom.

Arael watched Virgil leave, confused at his behavior. He thought about asking again when he went back to the bedroom, but he remembered that Virgil had recently been moved to another room for some reason... The room was closer to the Chancellor's chamber, so maybe she needed to keep a closer eye on him; it made Arael assume that Virgil had some kind of issue.

Once Virgil was gone, Arael looked over at the basin that he was crying over and spotted some red inside of it. He moved toward the basin to investigate, finding a few drops of fresh blood on the white marble. He looked back where Virgil had gone, and then to the basin in concern. Maybe he had a bloody nose or something? Virgil didn't seem like the type to let himself get beat up. Arael decided to rinse the blood down the drain with steaming water instead of just leaving it there. Blood wasn't the most pleasant thing to find in the basin, especially after it had dried. Arael watched it spiral down with the water until it disappeared, leaving the marble white again.

Once Arael turned off the water, he noticed that the showers were all off too and the washroom was very quiet. He sighed and then looked around before turning back to the foggy mirror. Arael snickered and then drew a sad Virgil face in the steam, before turning around to leave.

As Arael left the washroom, letting the door creek shut behind him, his steam art continued to frown, but it wasn't alone. A handprint slowly showed up and dragged across the mouth of the face, turning the frown into an unsettling smile...

CHAPTER ELEVEN
The Clues

The next day, all of the students immediately went to work on trying to find the clues again. It was a competition to them now, and some of them even made bets on who would find the treasures at the end of each set of clues. What they knew was that there were seven treasures total, each with their own sets of clues. Everyone had spent their entire break searching for those clues. It was tiring and annoying, but it was so hard to give up. Arael and Orias agreed to work with Schlimm, a girl named Blume, and her sister Kanin. It would be easier if they all could come up with ideas instead of just Arael and Orias. Maybe they would come up with things that they would never have thought of before.

They searched for the entire break with no luck, and they were running low on free time; it was getting late again and they were going to have to go back to class in the morning. Arael's group was sitting in Hammurabi the healer's infirmary, after being led there by a different clue that they were trying out. Arael had all of the clues written or sketched into his journal, so that it would be easier for them to recall.

"What if... What if it has something to do with the fountain outside? That has a statue of a famous healer on it, doesn't it?" Schlimm suggested.

Arael and Kanin shook their heads no.

"That statue isn't a healer, she's a mage," Kanin said.

Schlimm put his hand over his mouth in annoyance as he thought about it again. "Who knew that this would be so stinking hard...?" He mumbled.

"I think we should ask somebody," Orias said, looking at a symbol on a piece of cloth that provided their clue.

The symbol was supposedly a healer's symbol, but they hadn't seen it anywhere before.

"We already did," said Blume.

"Blaaaaah!!!" Orias yelled, plopping down on a chair. "One person can't be enough!"

"I bet stupid Virgil has already found one of the treasures..." Arael grumbled. "I hate him..."

Hammurabi was sitting in the corner, going over some health records that he'd written down about some of the students. He was a friendly old man with a bald head and round, wire glasses. He seemed crazy sometimes, but he always knew what he was talking about.

"No luck?" Hammurabi asked.

Arael looked in his direction. "No luck..." He answered.

Hammurabi walked across the room to grab something and then went back to his desk in the corner. "I think the answer is closer than you think," he said.

All of the teens perked up a bit.

"What do you mean? Do you know where the next clue is?" Arael asked.

Hammurabi smiled without a word and continued with his work, pushing his glasses further up the bridge of his nose. Arael stared at him for a moment as he was working, searching for anything that he could. Orias and the others did too. It seemed like they noticed it all at the same time; on the back of Hammurabi's bald head, there was a tattoo hidden against his dark skin, but it was the same as the symbol on the piece of cloth. All of the teens suddenly jumped up and ran to Hammurabi.

"It's you! It's you, isn't it!?" They said in excitement.

"Do you have the next clue, Hammurabi!? Is this your symbol!?" Orias asked.

Hammurabi laughed and nodded. "Yes, it's me!" He said. "Not a lot of students pause to ask any of the castle's staff about these things. Young Orias was closer to finding the answer than all of you!"

Orias smiled brightly at everyone, while Hammurabi reached into his pocket and pulled out a glass globe full of water, before dropping it into Orias's hands.

"This clue isn't what it represents, but what it says," Hammurabi said.

The teens cheered in excitement at finally finding the next clue. They stared at the globe for a moment to try and read what it said, but to their surprise, there was absolutely nothing written on it. They should've expected this, Mountainglaive didn't like to make things that easy.

"What the!?" Schlimm said.

They all looked at Hammurabi as he shrugged, having no more information that he was able to give them. They'd be cheating if he told them anything more.

"Well, does it speak?" Blume asked.

They stared at the globe and waited for it to say something, with no results.

"Hello, little buddy. Do you want to tell us where the next clue is?" Orias asked the globe.

They stared at it again and then Hammurabi laughed at their silliness. Obviously they were doing something wrong...

Schlimm stood up straight and stretched his arms. "Well, this has been fun... I'm going to bed, we all have class tomorrow. I guess we can meet up again afterwards..." He said. "Good night, guys."

Schlimm left the room and then Blume and Kanin decided to call it quits for the night as well. Orias and Arael still had the globe, wondering what it was supposed to do, but they decided that it was best to go to bed too. Hammurabi smiled at them as they waved goodbye and went on their way.

"I'm so excited now!" Orias said, jumping up and down as they walked down the hallway.

"Careful, don't drop it," Arael said.

Orias handed the globe to Arael to let him carry it. It didn't look like it did anything, it was just a ball full of water. It didn't even make any noise when they shook it. They came out into the vestibule and headed for the mirror that would carry them to their room. Arael continued to stare at the globe as he walked, while Orias wandered away from him.

"Maybe if you turn it a certain direction?" Arael said. He looked up, finding that Orias was not by his side anymore. "Orias?"

He turned around and spotted Orias, who had gone across the room, where a towering brick wall was placed, and Virgil was standing with him... Arael sighed in annoyance but decided to go to them anyway. Orias and Virgil were staring at the brick wall for some reason, so when Arael stopped next to them, he looked up at it too. There was nothing interesting that he could see, so he thought they were crazy.

"What're you looking at?" Arael asked.

"I don't know!" Orias shrugged. He looked to Virgil and shook his arm. "What are you looking at, Virgil?"

Virgil stood with his hands on his hips, and he wasn't taking his eyes away from the wall. "Oh, I'm just trying to figure out which of these bricks to take out first," he answered casually.

Arael raised an eyebrow at him. "Why?"

"It's the next task that goes with my clue," Virgil smiled.

"What!?" Arael said in surprise. "How many have you found!?"

Virgil paused to count on his fingers. It didn't look good for Arael... If Virgil had to think about how many he'd found, he had to have found a lot of them...

"Fifteen," Virgil answered.

Arael's eyes widened as his face turned bright red in embarrassment. It took him two days to find one clue! ...With help! What were they doing wrong!? Why was this boy so much better at everything than everybody else!? Arael felt ashamed of himself, so he hid the glass globe in a pocket on his surcoat.

"All by yourself!?" Orias asked.

"Yeah," Virgil answered.

Virgil reached into his pocket and then handed Orias a small wooden block that had rectangles burned into it on each side. Arael looked at the wooden block as Orias turned it in his hands. It didn't look like much to them.

"What makes you think this has anything to do with the brick wall?" Arael asked.

"I don't know. It just makes sense to me," Virgil shrugged, finally looking at Arael.

Arael noticed that Virgil's cheek was discolored, and there was a cut over it. He must have gotten beat up by somebody after all (either that or he ran into a wall.) Arael felt a little bit guilty for being mean to him, but he wasn't going to say anything; he only huffed as Orias handed the block back to Virgil.

"You see how each side has a different amount of burn marks missing?" Virgil rotated the block, showing them each side. "Those are the bricks that need to be removed... I believe."

Arael nodded, looking at the block. "That makes sense," he agreed, before pointing to a brick up above their heads. "So the first one would be that one there, right?"

Virgil looked at the brick wall and nodded. "Yeah, that's the one!" He said.

Arael and Orias were too short to reach it, but so was Virgil, even though he was taller than both of them. Arael was about to ask how they were going to get the brick out, but then Virgil decided to use his weird mage powers.

"Fluttari Motis," Virgil said with a flick of his wrist, commanding the brick to gently pull itself out of its place and float to the ground.

Once they figured out which bricks were next, Virgil did the same thing, pulling them all out of their places; it was amazing to watch the bricks hover all on their own. It certainly wasn't something that Arael and Orias were used to seeing. Virgil pulled the last brick out of its place, making a clicking noise that came from behind the wall. The boys all looked at each other in excitement and then the wall suddenly started to fold and open, making a doorway for them.

"Wow! Cool!" Orias exclaimed.

Once the brick wall was open, they stared into it for a moment, it was dark inside, and it looked like there were some steps that went down below.

"Should we go in?" Arael asked.

Virgil nodded with a smile and then cast Illustro, making his little ball of light appear so they could see in the dark. They walked down the steps, and found a good sized room placed at the bottom. The room had water in it, surrounding the path to the end. There were a few statues of old knights inside too. They walked to the end of the room, where there was a dusty old book, and a note left on top of it. Virgil held the light over the book, so they could read the note.

Arael read the note out loud, "'Dear students, congratulations, for you have come to the end of this hunt. You are one step closer to becoming part of our very own Legions. Please take the item that you have found to Chancellor Hofmeister, and you will be rewarded greatly.'"

The boys looked at each other in excitement. They had found the first treasure!!!

"You did it, Virgil!" Orias said, reminding Arael that it wasn't them that found any of this, it was Virgil.

"Yeah, good job, Virgil," Arael said, staring at the treasure. He didn't know what importance the book served anyway...

"Well, you two helped me, so it's only fair that you get some credit," Virgil said, picking up the book. "Come on, I think the Chancellor is still awake."

"But we just showed up, we didn't really do anything," Orias said.

"It doesn't matter, you still helped some," Virgil smiled.

Orias smiled back and thanked Virgil, then followed him. Arael stayed behind for a moment, staring at Virgil in shock. He couldn't believe it! Now he really felt like a horrible person. Virgil didn't owe him anything, yet he was letting him take credit in something that he didn't even help with. Arael wasn't even very nice to him. He was jealous of him if anything.

"Are you coming, Arael?" Virgil asked with a smile on his face.

Arael snapped out of it and nodded, finally following them to find the Chancellor. They went through the mirror in the vestibule to get to her chamber. The chamber was dim, with the light of only a single candle in the middle of the room, and it felt serene in there. Chancellor Hofmeister had a big fat pet rabbit named Lilou in her chamber that was always free to wander around. The grey rabbit hopped up to Orias and let him pick her up and pet her soft fur.

"Miss Hofmeister?" Virgil said, looking around.

"Yes, I'm here," they heard the Chancellor's voice.

In the corner of the room was a chair, where they saw the Chancellor stand up. She looked like a red ghost when she moved, and then she appeared to solidify. They weren't sure if their eyes were playing tricks on them or if it was her own doing, it was rather beautiful either way.

"What is it you seek, my children?" She asked with a comforting tone, while folding her hands in front of herself and smiling.

"Sorry to bother you ma'am, but we found one of the hidden treasures from your treasure hunt," Virgil said, holding the book out to her.

The Chancellor smiled even brighter, and then gently pushed the book back toward Virgil. "It's yours now," she said. "Your effort has been noticed, my children."

The boys looked at each other and then back to the Chancellor.

"So, the treasures at the end are prizes?" Orias asked.

The Chancellor nodded yes in reply. "I'm quite proud," she said, looking to Virgil as if she knew what he had done for Orias and Arael.

It was funny, she was always extra nice or extra proud when they were all in the same room together. It had to have meant something. Maybe she knew something that they didn't.

"Thank you, ma'am. I guess we'll be on our way then," Virgil said politely.

Virgil looked excited that they got to keep the book. It was obviously ancient, and it had strange words on it that he must've been able to understand. The book had to have years of information and spells in it.

The Chancellor looked at Virgil more closely and then brushed her thumb over the wound on his cheekbone. "What happened here?" She asked.

Virgil looked at her as she healed his cheek with her magic. "Nothing... It was just an accident," he said.

The Chancellor nodded and they all smiled as Orias put the rabbit down on the ground. The boys turned to leave through the mirror, and this time they came out near the washroom since it was passed everyone's bedtime again. Virgil held the book to his chest like it was a child's teddy bear.

"Thank you, both of you," Virgil said.

"No, thank you... The prize is all yours, since you're the one who did all the work," Arael said.

It was almost painful to say those words to him, and it was irritating. He didn't understand why he felt like being such a jerk to this poor boy. Arael put his hand in his pocket and rolled the glass globe around in his fingers, still disappointed that they took so long to find the stupid thing.

"Have you found anything yourselves?" Virgil asked, noticing that Arael was fidgeting with something in his pocket.

Arael cringed at the question but then slowly pulled the globe out to show him anyway. "Just one..." he said.

"We got it from Hammurabi! He said that it's not what it represents but what it says," Orias added.

Virgil's book floated into the air and then disappeared. That was something that a lot of the mages in Mountainglaive did. It was how they quickly put their things away. Their magic mentor, Lady Agnes, frequently did the same thing when she didn't need things. It was the same when they needed to get something, they just summoned it out of thin air.

"Can I see it?" Virgil asked, holding his hand out.

Arael sighed, "Sure..." Dropping the globe into Virgil's hand.

Virgil examined it for a moment, whispering Hammurabi's clue to himself that Orias had told him.

"It has to be a hot spring drop," Virgil quickly concluded.

Arael smacked himself in the forehead, he knew exactly what a hot spring drop was! Why didn't he recognize the thing? "I know what that is... You get it wet in hot water and it reveals words, right?" He said.

"Exactly," said Virgil.

"Let's do it now!" Orias said, taking the globe from Virgil and running to the washroom.

Arael and Virgil ran after him. This time there was nobody inside the room; the other students all went to bed earlier, since classes started early in the morning. Arael knew that he was going to regret staying up late, but he wasn't going to be able to sleep anyway, he was too worked up about the clues.

They watched as Orias put the globe into one of the basins and turned the hot water on, fogging up the mirror once again. They waited until the hot water finally caused the globe to change. It was quite the sight. The globe changed from clear to a foggy white color, while words appeared on the surface. Once it stopped changing, Orias turned the water off and reached for the globe.

"Careful, it'll be hot," Arael warned him.

"Oh! Right! Thanks, Arael," Orias said.

Orias covered his hands with the long fabric of his surcoat so the hot globe wouldn't burn him. He could still feel the warmth on his hands, but it didn't hurt. They examined the words on the globe, finding that it said 'Your answer lies within the enchanted shield.'

"The enchanted shield?" Orias asked.

"I guess somebody has an enchanted shield," Arael said.

Orias and Arael looked at Virgil for an answer, but he shrugged with no knowledge of an enchanted shield.

"I'm sure I can find out what this is talking about soon enough," Virgil said. "If you want me to continue to help you that is…"

Before Arael could answer, Orias did for them. Of course he excitedly accepted Virgil's help. Arael just had to calm himself down and quit being so jealous. He figured Virgil's strict father didn't give him much room for failure, so that was why he always succeeded at everything. Arael was glad that his own father wasn't very strict. He just had some normal house rules to keep him from losing his manners and responsibility.

Arael's gaze drifted to the foggy mirror, where he spotted a face drawn on it. He remembered that he'd drawn a face on the mirror the night before, but he thought that it was at a different basin… And this was a happy face, not a frowny one.

"Did you do that, Orias?" Arael asked, pointing to the mirror.

Orias stopped talking to Virgil and looked at the face on the mirror. "No," he answered. "I didn't see it there before. That's strange."

Virgil walked closer to the mirror to see the face. "I'm sure it's leftover from the last time somebody was here. These pictures stick around for a while after people draw them," he said, providing a logical explanation.

Orias put the globe into his pocket and decided to turn the hot water on in another basin. The steam floated about and fogged up the mirror above, just as it did over the other basin.

"What are you doing?" Arael asked.

"I don't know. Experimenting," Orias smiled.

There wasn't anything on the mirror where the steam was, they were just staring at nothing. Virgil and Arael weren't even sure what Orias was expecting to see. After a minute, there was still nothing, and the fog was starting to disappear from the mirror.

"I should get to bed," Virgil said. "Goodnight."

While Virgil turned to leave, Orias drew a happy face in the remaining fog, but to his surprise, another one showed up next to it. Arael saw this as well, he had no idea what to think of it! This was completely bizarre!

"What the!?" Orias exclaimed.

Virgil turned around to see the pictures on the mirror, walking back to Arael's side.

"Did- did you see that!?" Arael asked.

Orias looked at Arael and Virgil with wide eyes, and then Arael suddenly gasped, taking a step backwards. Arael had another vision; there was blood covering the floor and some horrible presence that he couldn't explain.

"Arael, are you alright?" Virgil asked, grabbing Arael's arm.

Arael glanced at Virgil and saw the startling figure of a Pneumati creature instead of the boy before him. Arael pulled away from him and accidentally fell backwards, hitting the floor.

"Pneumati!" Arael gasped, before the vision ended and he saw Virgil before him once again.

Virgil looked absolutely shocked. Arael had never seen his face like that before; he could've sworn that Virgil's heart had just leaped into his throat. Orias was staring between the two in confusion, uncertain of whether he was supposed to do something or not.

"Pneumati?" Virgil asked, with a horrified tone to his voice. "Wh- why did you say that?"

Arael stared at him in silence for a moment, stunned at what he'd just done. He scared himself. Why was he seeing these things!? "I- don't know," he finally answered. "I don't know! What's wrong with me!?"

Abruptly, every single one of the faucets in the washroom suddenly turned on, pouring hot water into the basins. Orias jumped back and stared at the running water as Virgil pulled Arael to his feet and held him protectively. They all stared in alarm as the steam fogged up the entire mirror. They wanted to run away, but they felt compelled to watch. Virgil and Arael briefly snapped out of it and ran to turn the faucets off, but as they grabbed the handles, the metal burned their hands. That had never happened before. The two clenched their fists in pain and retreated back to Orias as the basins started to overflow and pour hot water out onto the floor. The showers all turned on now too. Every drop of water was steaming hot and the floor was being flooded. Orias was frozen with fear as he stared at the water.

"Infra Therma!" Virgil shouted, freezing all of the water in the room.

The chaos stopped briefly, but the ice quickly melted. Virgil didn't understand why his spell didn't keep the water frozen! The room was becoming extremely hot, and the steam was making it hard for them to see.

"Let's get out of here!" Arael said, running for the door.

Orias didn't budge, so Virgil picked the smaller boy up and brought him to the door. Arael tried to open the door, but it was stuck!

"Come on!" Arael yelled, pounding on the door.

"Let me!" Virgil said, gently pushing Arael aside.

Virgil reared back and swung his fist in a punching motion. He didn't even have to say the spell this time. A concussive blast shot from him and into the door, cracking it slightly; but then the blast somehow came back at him and smashed him against the tile wall that was separating the showers from the basins. Arael watched in astonishment as Virgil recovered quickly, he was glad that the boy was uninjured, but hitting the tile still couldn't have been fun. Virgil shook his little mishap off and went to Orias, grabbing ahold of him protectively as he did with Arael earlier. Orias was still frozen, staring at the mirrors. Arael started to kick the door where Virgil had cracked it, having not much luck.

"Somebody help!" Arael yelled.

Arael looked back at Virgil and Orias as they watched the foggy mirror in horror. Arael's eyes widened when he saw words were being written on the foggy mirrors, and then more and more continued to appear as if somebody was writing from the other side of the mirror.

The unknown finished writing its message; 'The darkness will prevail.'

"Virgil, try your spell again!" Arael said.

Virgil turned to Arael in panic and let go of Orias to do as Arael had said. He did the same thing as before, shooting a concussive blast at the door, but this time he moved before the blast reflected back at him. Arael kicked the door next, finally breaking it! They stumbled out into the hallway and then started running to get to the mirror that could take them to the Chancellor. Virgil held Orias's wrist, making sure that he was still with them. When they reached the mirror, it suddenly shattered into pieces, shooting shards of broken glass at them.

Arael blocked his face with his hands while Virgil protected Orias from harm. The glass cut Arael's hands and arms, but he didn't have much time to think about it. They continued down the hallway and found that all of the mirrors were exploding, rendering them useless. Suddenly, someone came flying down the hallway and startled them, but once they saw who it was, they were slightly relieved. It was Sir Cornelius! But what could he do?

"What's going on down here!?" Cornelius asked in concern.

"There's something attacking us!" Orias finally spoke.

"The washroom! It was in there!" Arael said.

"Stay here!" Said Cornelius, before drawing his sword and running down the hall to the washroom.

"Don't!" Arael said, but it was too late, Sir Cornelius was already set on his mission.

Arael remembered the blood on the floor in his vision, right before all of this had happened. He only hoped that it didn't mean anything. Orias gripped Virgil's black and gold surcoat like a toddler, with tears running down his cheeks. Sometimes Arael forgot that Orias was only thirteen and still acted like a child. They all felt like crying though. Orias was just the only one letting it out. They waited until they heard someone else running up the hall behind them. This time it was Enzo, followed by the magic mentor Lady Agnes, Sir Gwenael, the Chancellor, and a few concerned students. Everyone was in their pajamas, with no shoes on.

"What's happening!?" Enzo asked.

"Sir Cornelius went into the washroom! There's something bad in there! It flooded the floor with hot water and wrote on the mirror!" Arael explained, pointing toward the washroom.

Enzo turned and saw the broken mirror nearby, and then he looked up the hall and ran to the washroom. He had his sword with him at least. Everyone watched as Enzo got to the washroom entrance and stopped, holding his sword out in front of himself defensively. He bravely snuck in to search for whatever evil had caused this chaos. Next they saw him back out and pause where he was, staring into the room with a look of dismay.

"What is it, Dante!? What do you see!?" The Chancellor asked in concern, running down the hall to be with him.

Everyone else decided to follow her and stopped at the entrance of the boy's washroom. Arael, Virgil and Orias gasped in horror when they saw what was before them. The floors were free of water now, without a drop to be seen. But what horrified everyone was the blood stained tile, surrounded by broken glass. The entire mirror in the washroom had shattered into thousands of pieces, and on the floor was Sir Cornelius in a pool of his own blood. It wasn't clear if the glass or something else had killed him, but one thing was for sure, he was dead...

Arael had only ever seen death like this once; death right in front of him. He'd always been protected from it, but he knew that it was everywhere. All that he could do was stare. Nobody could believe it.

"Is he dead?" Orias asked in panic. "Chancellor, is he dead!?"

Ego had pushed through the crowd to see, coming up next to Virgil. She was shocked too. This place was supposed to be safe! What was happening here!?

The Chancellor looked at the kids and then put her arms out to her sides. "Come on now, I want you all to go back to your rooms," she said. "You three as well," she pointed to Virgil, Arael and Orias. "I'm sorry you all had to see this. Go on now, we'll take care of this and then we'll speak of it in the morning."

The students took one last look at what was left of Sir Cornelius and then did as the Chancellor said, making their way back to their rooms. Hammurabi caught up with the group a bit too late, and followed the three teens to fix their wounds once they found somewhere to sit down. Orias was still crying, but Arael had a feeling that it wasn't the last time something like this would happen.

He reflected back on the vision that he'd gotten right before all of this... The blood splattered on the washroom floor... These visions were becoming real now and he was worried.

CHAPTER TWELVE
Dreamwalker

The next day, everyone went to their classes like normal. The boy's washroom was cleaned up and fixed, but nobody wanted to go in there. What had happened was still a mystery. Arael didn't even want to think about the clues that he was hunting for anymore. He felt sick, and it was difficult to concentrate in the classes.

Arael listened to the apothecary, Francesco, talking about herbs. This was an important class to listen to if Arael ever needed to make some medicine, but it was not interesting at the moment... The healers and mages were made for this class anyway; Arael wasn't sure what he was yet, but he certainly wasn't one of those two options... At the beginning of the class, Francesco informed everyone that Sir Cornelius was no longer going to be in Mountainglaive, and Sir Enzo would teach combat until they found somebody else to do it. He didn't tell anyone that Sir Cornelius was dead, however... He didn't even give anyone any information on what exactly happened, only that he was not around anymore. Arael figured that it was probably to protect the younger kids.

Nobody that Arael knew very well was in this class, so he was left alone to think about the last night's events. He really didn't want to think about it, but he couldn't stop his brain. He was spinning his charcoal pencil around, resting his cheek in his hand. His journal was sitting in front of him, with new drawings of the washroom mirror, and the things that he'd seen the night before. He looked up at Francesco for a moment, and then spotted Chancellor Hofmeister standing nearby. She was looking straight at Arael. Arael lifted his head and looked at her as she smiled and gestured for him to come to her. He looked around for a moment, and then hesitantly got up from his seat and went straight to the Chancellor. The Chancellor smiled at him and brought him away from the classroom.

"I'm sorry to interrupt you, Mister Keon... I wanted to speak with you for a moment," said the Chancellor.

Arael looked at her and simply nodded, following her to her chamber. It was a much longer walk now, because all of the mirrors in the castle had mysteriously shattered into pieces during the night's events. It happened all at the same time too. Everyone was still trying to find out what had caused that. When Arael and the Chancellor got to her chamber, Arael saw that Orias, Virgil and Ego were all waiting for them. Orias was petting Lilou again,

Virgil was reading the ancient book that he got from the treasure hunt, and Ego was examining some chunks of amber on the walls that had fairies stuck in them. They must've been there because of last night... But Ego wasn't there until the end, so Arael wasn't sure why she was waiting in the chamber.

"So..." The Chancellor started, getting everyone's attention. "None of you are in any trouble... But I would like you all to tell me what exactly you saw last night."

The teens all looked at each other and then Arael started, "First something drew a face in the fog that was on the mirror in the boy's washroom, just after Orias drew a face... Next all of the faucets in the room got turned on by an unknown force." He flipped through his journal to show the Chancellor his sketches of the event.

"Then we tried to escape," Orias added.

Virgil nodded. "Once the entire mirror was fogged up," his voice cracked at the memory, "The words 'The darkness will prevail' showed up on the mirror. Orias and I saw it physically being written out. After that, we escaped the room and ran into Sir Cornelius, who decided to go into the washroom himself."

The boys looked to Ego, curious of what she'd seen.

"In the girl's washroom, I saw a man walking around in the mirror, but when I checked the room, there was nobody there. After that, a face was drawn in the fog on the mirror like what you guys saw, and then the entire mirror shattered. I ran and then heard you guys making a commotion..." Ego explained.

The boys' eyes widened. They were almost relieved that they weren't the only ones that had seen crazy things, but it was also terrifying that this had happened in multiple places at the same time. Arael thought about the vision that he had again, wondering if he should say something about that, but he felt like they'd think he was insane.

The Chancellor took a moment to think about this. "Dieudonne..." She muttered. "He must be planning something... Unless this is something else..." When she was done talking to herself, the Chancellor looked to Arael. She knew that he had something more that he wasn't telling. "Is there something else, Mister Keon?"

Arael looked to her, hesitant to answer... "N-nothing ma'am..."

The Chancellor smiled softly, "Please tell. You can't hide these things from me, child."

Arael's stomach felt sick; he didn't want to say what had been happening to him, but it looked like he had no choice now. He was afraid of what it could mean. The other teens sat quietly, waiting for him to answer the Chancellor's question; he wished they weren't there to hear it, but they wanted an explanation as well. Especially Virgil, since Arael had screamed at him about the Pneumati that he'd seen in the washroom.

"Well ma'am," Arael started, "I..." He paused. "Since Breckenridge was attacked, I've been having strange dreams about the Pneumati. Just recently I've had brief visions during the day. They feel so real... I don't understand what is happening."

Arael glanced over at Virgil as he put his hands over his mouth and looked to the floor, with a slight gasp. Arael wasn't sure if he was shocked at what he said, or if it was something else that had to do with it; it made Arael's heart sink even further than it already was. Orias and Ego just stared, they didn't know anything about it.

The Chancellor put her hand over her heart and then hugged Arael. Arael just stood there. He wasn't sure what anybody's actions meant. He thought of the worst though... Maybe he was crazy, or maybe he had something wrong with his brain. Maybe he was going to die! It could've been anything! The Chancellor stopped hugging him and then looked at him, holding onto his shoulders. Arael was holding back the urge to cry.

"This isn't a bad thing, young Arael," the Chancellor smiled, "But, it is indeed very rare."

Orias looked between the Chancellor and Arael in confusion. "What is it?" He asked.

Before the Chancellor could answer, Virgil did instead, "He's a Dreamwalker."

Virgil still looked concerned, and he was still staring at the floor. Arael looked to Virgil, he'd heard of a Dreamwalker, but not enough to know exactly what it was. Virgil's reaction was making him nervous, he almost wanted to tell him to quit it.

"What's a Dreamwalker, ma'am?" Arael asked the Chancellor.

The Chancellor smiled, happy to answer his question, "A Dreamwalker is able to get information about the future, through dreams... Dreamwalkers are also able to enter other people's minds, more easily through dreams. It sounds like you are quite the strong one, but it takes a long time for the ability to work smoothly and be controlled... In most cases the abilities of a Dreamwalker are unlocked through big changes in their lives."

Arael stared at the Chancellor with wide eyes, he wasn't sure if he was excited about this or terrified. He knew exactly what the huge change was that unlocked this 'power' though... The attack on his home and leaving his father behind, to go to a place that was completely unfamiliar hit him pretty hard...

"So... Is that good?" Arael asked.

"Very... If you make it good," said the Chancellor.

"Cool, Arael! You have superpowers!" Orias said in excitement, jumping up and down.

Arael smiled at Orias, but his smile faded when he thought about his most recent vision again. "So... Right before we were attacked in the washroom... I got a quick vision of blood splashing on the floor, right where Sir Cornelius was found... And then, when I looked at Virgil, I saw a Pneumati, and then it was done..." Arael explained.

The Chancellor looked away from him for a moment, sad about Cornelius's death. "That was certainly a vision of the future," she looked at Arael once again and smiled warmly, "But do not blame yourself for this. You didn't know. No one is to blame but the entity that caused this."

Virgil finally looked up, Arael wondered what his deal was. Maybe Virgil was finally jealous of something that

Arael could do this time. Wouldn't that be great? Now Arael had something to be proud of, instead of being jealous of Mister Know-It-All. Arael's self-pride was starting to get the best of him now... At least he felt better...

"Now..." Said the Chancellor. "I apologize for taking you from your classes. You may be on your way now. Though, I would like you to report to me when you have more visions, Mister Keon."

Arael nodded yes and then the teens all turned to leave.

"Oh. Orias, I would like you to stay," the Chancellor said, stopping Orias upon remembering something.

Orias and Arael looked at each other and then waved goodbye before Arael exited the room. Arael was wondering what she wanted with Orias now! He would make sure to ask when he saw him next. Arael looked at his hands, feeling like he had to make sure he was still the same person. He felt different now that he knew about this new ability that he possessed. It was scary but great at the same time. Every time something good happened to Arael, he wished that he could tell his father about it. His father would surely cry those proud parent tears. Every time Arael thought of his father though, he was always reminded of how much he missed him... Someday he would get to show him everything he'd learned, all of his accomplishments and even talk his ears off about all of the new experiences.

CHAPTER THIRTEEN
The Rider

Orias followed Chancellor Hofmeister outside, to the field behind the castle. Enzo was training another class out in the grassy, brown field near the arch that led to the maze. Orias made sure to wave to everyone as he walked by. Schlimm was there with Enzo, so Orias waved to them extra hard. Orias didn't pick favorites very often, but Sir Enzo was his favorite knight. Enzo was like a cool uncle in Orias's mind.

Even though Orias was happy most of the time, his life back at home wasn't quite as happy. His parents had died from a terrible sickness when he was nine years old. After that, he lived with a family that owned many animals, and a large farm. The family made him sleep in the barn, but Orias was okay with it since all of the animals slept there too. He loved animals more than anything... Whenever the Pneumati came by, Orias was always able to slip past them by hiding in the barn. He had a few close calls though, when the Pneumati came to steal some of the animals. It always broke Orias's heart when he saw them take his four legged friends...

Eventually the Pneumati took the family's three children, leaving them with only Orias. They became angry with Orias because of this and treated him badly. Orias understood why they felt that they needed to do it though... His heart was always too good. During his time with the family, he often had to go out to run errands for them, so that they wouldn't have any chances of running into the Pneumati. It was ironic what happened really... It was an errand run that saved Orias from the night that the Pneumati attacked all of the villages in the lands. The wife was sick, so the husband sent him out in the middle of the night to go get medicine; still in his pajamas, Orias did as he was told and was picked up by Sir Gwenael just as the Pneumati attacked his home.

Orias was happier than he'd ever been now that he was at Mountainglaive. He had his own bed, friends, good food, and he considered the knights to be parent figures. Chancellor Hofmeister was like everyone's mother... Orias looked up ahead, to where the Chancellor was taking him and spotted that little old, stone building that housed the dragon eggs inside. He wondered why they were going back to that place when he was specifically told not to...

"Why are we going to the dragon house, Miss?" Orias asked politely.

The Chancellor smiled at him. "I know that you were told not to go back here, but that was because the dragon wasn't ready to hatch yet. But now it is, and it called you," she explained.

"The dragon called me?" Orias asked.

"Yes. You are to be its rider," said the Chancellor. "You are the first rider of the year to be called by a dragon."

Orias thought about this for a moment. He was going to get his own dragon! More importantly, he knew the four types of great knights. Not everyone was called to a type, which meant that if he was a rider, then he was surely more likely to be in one of the legions. There were the helms, the mages, the protectors and the riders. There were healers as well, but they were meant for support; they were assigned to random legions sometimes. He'd never heard of a dragon rider though, only ones that rode horses and direwolves. Horse riders really weren't that special, anybody could ride a horse... All riders had special connections with animals though, which explained a lot about Orias.

"Are dragon riders rare?" Orias asked.

"Oh yes," answered the Chancellor, as they reached the stone building. "One of our riding mentors, Felix has a beautiful dragon of his own, and he takes care of all of the other dragons at Mountainglaive."

Orias watched as she opened the door with ease, using her magic powers to do so. Orias wasn't sure if the Chancellor was a mage, or something completely different. She seemed too graceful and ghostlike to be a mage, but she was certainly magical. Once the door was open, she nudged him into the building, letting him take the lead.

Orias saw the green glow once again, where the dragon egg was waiting. He went to the egg, while the Chancellor watched from the door. Orias stared at the egg for a moment, and then placed his hand on top of it, feeling its warmth. The egg was vibrating, tickling Orias's fingers. He giggled at it, and then the egg suddenly made a loud snapping noise, and a large crack shot down the center. Orias pulled away from it in concern. He thought he'd broken it, but then he remembered that the Chancellor said that it was going to hatch.

The egg cracked again and again, until pieces started to fall off of it. The glowing stopped and the sounds of the egg pieces falling could be heard through the darkness. Orias waited until the egg stopped breaking and all there was, was silence. After a moment, the green glow came back, but this time, it came from a tiny baby dragon that was sitting on top of the eggshells. The little dragon was beautiful. Its scales were black, with that green glow coming from them, and its belly was white. Its wings were still delicate since it was only a hatchling, but it would soon become big and strong.

Orias was so happy when he saw the dragon. There were no words that he could get out, he could only smile and stare at it. The dragon stared back at him and made a tiny squeaking noise. It didn't seem aggressive, it wasn't even scared. It was just curious. Orias slowly approached the dragon and bent down to see it. The dragon looked at him and squeaked again. The little dragon made Orias so happy that his eyes started to tear up. When he reached out to the dragon, it walked to his hand and climbed onto his arm and up to his shoulder, immediately becoming comfortable with him. The dragon rubbed its warm, scaly face against Orias's cheek, like a cat would. Orias giggled at the dragon and rubbed his finger against its forehead before looking to the Chancellor. The Chancellor was happy for him. She smiled so hard that her cheeks ached.

"I love her!" Orias said. "It's like she's talking to me when she squeaks, and I can- understand her. Is that normal?"

The Chancellor nodded, "Riders have a special connection with their companions. She understands you as well as you understand her."

"She's mine? Can I name her?" Orias asked as he walked back to the Chancellor.

"Of course," the Chancellor answered.

Orias smiled even more. Now he was definitely happier than he had ever been in his entire life. "Okay! Her name is Nerida! I'll take good care of her forever!" Orias said in excitement, hugging the little dragon.

Orias followed the Chancellor out of the dragon house and she made sure the door was shut behind them. When they were out in the field, Orias saw Enzo's class wrapping up for the next class. Orias dashed across the field, he wanted to show everyone his new dragon!

"Sir Enzo! Sir Enzo!" Orias called. "Look at my dragon, Sir Enzo!"

Enzo turned around in surprise, as his class looked at Orias in confusion. Orias stopped in front of Enzo and held the dragon up like a puppy for him to see.

"I'm a dragon rider, Sir Enzo! Her name is Nerida!" Orias said, so excited that he almost forgot to breathe.

Enzo raised his eyebrows and then looked to the Chancellor and back to Orias. "That's incredible!" He said. Enzo brushed his graying hair away from his face so he could see the dragon better, and kneeled down to Orias's height. "Amazing! She's beautiful!" He exclaimed, touching the dragon's cute little foot.

All of the students in Enzo's class surrounded them so they could see the dragon. They were all fascinated with her. They asked all kinds of questions that Orias really didn't know the answers to yet, but he happily told them about what he did know.

After a few minutes, Enzo finally stood up. "Alright, alright, you all need to get to your next classes," he said.

The students were a bit disappointed, but they listened anyway. Schlimm congratulated Orias on his way out, and some girls even waved at him.

"Bye, Schlimm!" Orias said.

"We're all proud of you, Orias," Enzo smiled, patting him on the back.

Orias looked up at Enzo and smiled. "Hey! My next class is with you, isn't it? Since you're the combat mentor now?" He said.

"Indeed I am," Enzo answered. "I'll walk you to the classroom, how about that?"

Orias nodded yes, and then ran to the Chancellor to give her a hug. "Thank you, Miss," Orias said before letting go of her and leaving with Enzo.

The Chancellor and Enzo smiled at each other before they went their separate ways. Orias followed Enzo back to the castle, petting his new dragon the whole time. The dragon squeaked at him a few times, and Orias understood what she was trying to tell him. She somehow caught the last clue that Orias, Arael and Virgil had found on the hot spring drop. The dragon was quick to lock minds with Orias, it was quite an amazing thing. Nerida squeaked a few more times, drawing Orias's attention to a shield that was fastened to Sir Enzo's back by a leather strap. Orias remembered the clue that the drop had given them, 'your answer lies within the enchanted shield.'

"Sir Enzo!" Orias said loudly.

Enzo stopped walking and turned around. "What is it, boy!?" He asked in alarm.

"Is your shield enchanted!?" Orias asked.

Enzo looked at him for a moment, realizing that there was nothing concerning that Orias was yelling at him about. Enzo's face softened and then he answered Orias's question, "Yes, indeed it is."

Orias smiled at the dragon on his shoulder and then looked back to Enzo. "Do you have a clue!?" He asked.

Enzo smiled and then took his shield off and offered it to Orias. "Why don't you find out?"

Orias took the shield in excitement; it was much heavier than he thought it would be. Enzo must've been really strong to have to carry this shield, his sword and his armor around. Orias looked at the inside of the shield, where there was something written on it. It said 'My love will always protect you. We are a set, like this shield, and my sword. As long as the set is complete, the shield will protect you. Dante, you are the shield to my sword and my love for you will never die.' On the other side, were the words that enchanted the shield, 'Let my love be your shield,' written in another language, and a picture that looked like a double trinity knot, connected with hearts.

Orias looked up at Enzo when he finished reading, and Nerida squeaked. "Do I have to find the sword that this is talking about?" Orias asked. "Who's the lady that wrote this?"

Enzo smiled and shrugged, pretending that he didn't know. Orias smiled at him, it was easy to know that the answer to the first question was yes. Enzo took the shield back and then they continued on. Orias was excited to tell Arael about all that he'd discovered! Or maybe... Or maybe he should keep the clue that he found to himself; then, maybe everyone would quit doubting him and thinking that he was stupid. Orias looked at Nerida, who clearly agreed with him. Orias felt more confident than ever now! It was like he had just found a part of himself that he'd lost.

CHAPTER FOURTEEN

News to Me

Arael was standing in the room for combat class, waiting for Enzo to arrive. He was always a little bit early since he had no stops to make in between classes, even though others did for some reason, maybe for goofing off. He, Virgil, Orias, and five other kids were always the first to arrive. This time though, Orias hadn't shown up yet. Arael wondered what the Chancellor needed from him. He looked around, watching the doors for Orias.

Arael was still excited about what he'd just learned about his dreamwalking abilities. His mind was running rampant about all of the possibilities that his power could unlock. He wanted to rub it in everybody's faces, but that would definitely be rude of him. He clutched the hilt of his sword that he'd gotten from a case in the room. All of the students got special cases for their weapons, so that they could keep them in the combat room. Arael wished that he could carry his sword around all the time, especially after what had happened in the boy's washroom... That could become possible if he ever became a knight. All of the elder knights around Mountainglaive carried their weapons with them at all times.

After a while, most of the other kids that were supposed to be in combat class had arrived. Arael looked at the entrance again, when finally, he saw Enzo and Orias come in. Enzo walked away from Orias and went to the dueling stage to get ready. Once Orias saw Arael, he waved and ran to him. Arael was surprised when he saw the little dragon on Orias's shoulder!

"Where did you get that!?" Arael asked.

"The Chancellor brought me back to that stone building with the dragon eggs and told me that I'm a rider! A dragon rider!" Orias said in excitement.

"What!? You are a dragon rider!?" Arael asked in astonishment.

Arael couldn't believe that Orias was actually a dragon rider! That was a one in a million chance! Why him? Although, Arael had just found out that he had a special ability, so he was in no position to be jealous. He was actually impressed this time.

"Isn't it great!?" Orias asked. "Her name is Nerida!"

Arael smiled and rubbed the dragon's chin with his finger. "Hello, Nerida," he said.

Just then, Sir Enzo called attention to the class, getting them to look up at him. Orias and Arael walked up to the edge of the dueling stage, next to Ego. Ego was always by herself since everyone was afraid of her; in a way, it was sad. Orias and Arael were afraid of her too, so they kept their distance. Really, they felt a little bit bad that she was always alone, but it wasn't like she welcomed anybody's presence. Orias and Arael didn't really have anybody that they hung out around either, nor did Virgil. They were all different compared to the other students, they were certainly the peculiar type, but they didn't think much of it.

"Well students, I'm sure you've all been informed of Sir Cornelius's absence from here on out, and I know that we're all quite hurt by this," Enzo started, when somebody that they had never seen before walked up onto the dueling stage and stopped next to him. Enzo continued, "I was called to replace him for the time being, until we have a new combat mentor. There is a new knight that has traveled all the way here from Jollenbeck, to learn what he needs to know as quickly as possible in order to teach you, and I'd like you to meet him..." He gestured to the man next to him. "This here is your new combat mentor-to-be, Sir Albern Adonis."

The man next to Enzo waved stiffly to the students, with a slight attempt at smiling. Sir Adonis looked like he'd been through many battles and won them. Arael and Orias looked at each other and back to the man who was going to be the new combat mentor. Sir Adonis looked much tougher than Cornelius ever was; they were afraid to know what he had in store for them.

"Good day. I'm pleased to be here to teach you and more importantly, learn from you," said Sir Adonis, nodding his head.

The kids weren't sure what to do, so they all clapped skeptically. Enzo looked at Adonis; the kids could tell by his facial expression that he was just as unsure of this guy as they were.

"Ahem... Sir Adonis is going to watch us today, to try and get a feel for what the classes will be like, so don't be uncomfortable when he watches you. He's learning too," Enzo explained. "Righto! Let us get started, shall we?"

CHAPTER FIFTEEN
Long Days

After about a week, Sir Adonis had taken control of the combat class, leaving Enzo to his own job. The first day wasn't quite as bad as the students had expected. Sir Adonis was actually an okay guy then, but when they started getting more into it, that's when things started to get tough. Sir Adonis didn't seem to have much patience for his students. He gave them a one day grace period, but after that, he expected them all to be experts right off the top. Everyone dreaded the combat class now... No matter what they did, Sir Adonis somehow found a way to shut them down. What the students were supposed to be doing was dueling each other with wooden versions of the weapons that they had created, but Sir Adonis made sure to replace one side of the duel with himself. He insisted that if they didn't use real weapons, they'd become soft and unfit for battle, but after a few of the students complained to the Chancellor, that didn't go on for long.

Everyone always came out with bumps and bruises. It was exhausting. Arael was happy that combat class was always his last of the day, or else he would've collapsed and not been able to continue on. Poor Orias never stood a chance against Sir Adonis. After a while he just quit trying and ended up disappearing halfway through every class. Arael had no idea where he was going, but he didn't blame him for leaving. He just wished that he didn't leave him behind... Riders really weren't built for hardcore combat like this. Sir Adonis was of the protector class, like Sir Gwenael, and Ego. Ego was the best match for him so far.

For the first time ever, Arael saw Virgil get his butt handed to him. Nobody was ever able to even match Virgil's skill, but Sir Adonis could do it easily. He was able to mirror everyone's moves and use them against them. Virgil got beat up the most out of anyone, because Adonis said that he saw 'potential' in him, since he was such a good fighter. For such a delicate looking person, Virgil was able to take a beating. The first few times it was funny, but then everyone started feeling bad for him. Some kids continued to laugh at him when he got beat up. Arael found that Virgil did not take losing well; he was becoming frustrated with Adonis. Every time Adonis beat him, he refused to give up even though he was already down and out. Nobody had ever seen the cool and collected smart kid like this. Once, Virgil pushed himself so far that when he got knocked to the ground for the last time, some of the knights had to come and drag him to Hammurabi, not before he tried to insist that he wanted to try again...

Ego always put up a good fight, but she gave up quickly, since she didn't like being humiliated more than once. Sir Adonis was by far the toughest knight in the entire castle... Whenever it was Arael's turn, he had to block more than fight. Whenever he tried to land a blow on Sir Adonis, was always his downfall. He was relieved every time it was over, because fighting with Sir Adonis sucked. Everyone was always relieved when the day was done...

The last duel of the day was about to take place, which was Virgil versus Sir Adonis... It was going to be painful to watch. Once again, Orias had gone to wherever it was that he disappeared to. Arael had just finished his own duel; Adonis kicked the back of his leg pretty hard, so it was difficult for him to stand now. He was good at dealing with pain though, or at least hiding it.

Virgil huffed and took a wooden staff – which was the closest to his swallow wand that he could get – and then he stood across from Sir Adonis, ready to fight. Arael could always see on his face that he was sure he was going to win, but of course, that never happened. Arael wished he could use his Dreamwalker powers to figure out what Sir Adonis was going to do, then maybe everyone could cheat him. Arael watched as Adonis stood comfortably with his wooden sword at his side, looking at Virgil like he was nothing. He looked bored more than anything.

Virgil was mad, but he was trying to be confident that he would win. "This time. This time for sure," he told himself.

Sir Adonis began the match and then they went after each other. Virgil attacked first – he never attacked first; he was getting reckless, since he was fed up with Adonis beating him all the time. If anything, Sir Adonis's approach was making the kids even worse at combat. They weren't going to learn anything if all that they did was fail. Sir Adonis was unbeatable!

Adonis dodged Virgil's attack and kicked him in the back to try and make him fall. Virgil turned around and attacked again, missing, so the next thing he did was wait for Adonis to attack. Virgil was able to hold up for a longer time than most of the other kids, but whatever he did just wouldn't bring the man down. Arael watched eagerly, he actually wanted Virgil to win. He cheered him on in his head. The suspense of the fight was hard to take. Finally, Virgil had him, knocking Adonis off balance for a moment. He took the window of opportunity to go for one last blow. All of the students leaned forward and held their breath, eager to see Adonis lose.

Unfortunately, Adonis pulled a move out of nowhere and knocked Virgil in the face with the wooden sword. Virgil flew a few feet before hitting the floor. The students sighed in disappointment, while Virgil got up and tossed his staff on the ground before storming off of the dueling stage. Arael was surprised; Virgil must've been really angry now, he never behaved that way... A few kids pushed and laughed at Virgil as he left the room, making fun of him like a bunch of jerks. Arael wondered what made those guys so great... They never did anything impressive, so they were in no position to make fun of anybody.

Arael sighed and put his wooden sword away before heading for the exit. Everybody was on their way to supper now. Arael saw Virgil in the hallway, as he went into the neutral washroom; the poor guy's nose was gushing with blood. He was a huge mess. The blood made him look like he had a red moustache and his teeth were all stained with it too. Luckily Arael didn't have any blood to clean up this time, but he did many times before...

While Arael was walking, Ego caught up with him. "Hey, Arael," she said.

Arael looked at her in surprise, this was a first. Ego never tried to talk to anybody unless she was starting a fight. "Hi," he replied.

"Where has your friend been?" Ego asked.

"I don't know," Arael shrugged. "He gave up on combat class a while ago, he hasn't told me where he's been disappearing to."

Ego nodded and continued down the hall with Arael. Combat class was making all of the kids depressed, it was sad. Sir Adonis said that life as a knight would always be that tough, but Arael wasn't so sure about that; people like Enzo and Sir Gwenael seemed laid back enough.

Nobody else had made things this tough. Enzo told them the cold hard truth all the time and it wasn't nearly as bad.

When Arael and Ego got to the dining hall, they quickly spotted Orias, who was sitting at the table already, with his dragon sitting in front of him.

"Orias!" Arael said, sitting down next to him.

"How was class?" Orias asked, as Ego sat down at his other side.

"The same as usual. Virgil is getting real angry with Adonis. You should see it," Arael said. "Where have you been?"

Orias shrugged. He was being awful quiet. That was very unlike him. Arael was about to ask another question, but then they heard the Chancellor call for everyone's attention. All of the students looked toward the end of the room, where the Chancellor stood at the round table with all of the knights, including Sir Adonis...

"Good evening my children," the Chancellor started. "I'm pleased to announce that all of the treasures that I've hidden around the castle for you have been found!" All of the kids looked at each other in surprise. Arael was shocked! He'd forgotten all about those clues and treasures since Sir Adonis came along! The Chancellor continued to speak, "I'd like to announce all who found the treasures, and congratulate them on their success!" She opened up a scroll that had a list of the students who found the items on it. Arael was glad that he was on the list at least once... When the Chancellor began to read the list, Orias shrunk down a bit. "The first students to find one of the treasures were Fromm Flink, Belshazzar Aziz, and Erna Jutta, who found the Globe of King Ottimo."

Everyone clapped and cheered for the three who found the first treasure. Arael was sure that Virgil's name would show up first. Though, he was finding things on his own, and he wasn't the only smart kid in the castle. Fromm, Belshazzar and Erna were about his level, so it made sense.

"Next were Virgil Capello, Arael Keon and Orias Megalos, who found the great mage Thema's spell book. Once again, Virgil Capello, who found the Aegis crystal. Next, Orias Megalos, who found the great ax of Lord Zander—"

Arael's eyes widened in surprise; he was expecting Virgil's extra find, but not Orias's! He looked at Orias, waiting for an explanation. Even Ego was surprised. Orias was slouched over, looking at the dragon.

"Okay, okay..." Orias said, getting uncomfortable with everyone's staring eyes. "I was looking for the treasures the whole time I was away from combat class..."

"What!? By yourself!?" Arael asked in surprise.

"Well, Nerida helped me at first, but then I did it myself," Orias answered.

"You cheated then?"

"No! Not really because I already had a good idea of what the clues meant, but she pushed me to pursue them!"

"But how!?"

"Maybe I'm smarter than you think I am, Arael!? I just don't work well under pressure!" Orias exclaimed. "I talked to Virgil and found out that he beat us to that first clue that we tried to find; it was the one that was supposed to be behind the curtain in Sir Gwenael's classroom. So I was right about it. That was the one that led to his book."

Arael and Ego continued to look at Orias in surprise. Arael almost couldn't believe it. He felt like Orias was making all of this up, but the Chancellor had just announced his name, so it had to be true.

"Wait, so if I wasn't yelling at you in the maze thing, then we probably would've gotten a better score?" Ego asked.

"No offense, but I think anyone would've gotten a bad score if you were yelling at them. We don't even know what exactly that score was though," Orias said.

That dragon was either making Orias smarter or more open to say what was floating around in his skull. Arael wasn't sure if he liked it or not. It was really strange. Everybody had been changing in some way. Arael sort of wished that everything would go back to the way it was a few weeks ago – though, he wasn't one to welcome change anyway.

"Listen to the Chancellor, I found the last treasure too," Orias said.

Just as Orias said, the Chancellor announced his name again. The last treasure was the pendant of Zita, which Arael had noticed around the dragon's neck as soon as he heard the name. What a weird place to put a valuable pendant; around a dragon's neck... A baby dragon's neck! The Chancellor wouldn't have let him have it, if it was that important though, so Arael guessed it was fine where it was.

"Wow, you're on fire," Ego said, a bit unsure of what she was saying.

Arael nodded. "I'm impressed," he said through his teeth.

Orias smiled at them now, that was the normal Orias. He even greeted the Cocos when they came to give everyone their food. The students were still cheering in excitement, and some of them came to congratulate Orias before sitting back down to eat.

Toward the end of suppertime, Arael saw Virgil walking by himself after he'd finished eating. It was clear that he wasn't feeling that great. He was probably on his way to bed. Before Arael could turn his attention back to his food, he saw two guys get up and follow Virgil out of the dining hall. He knew that those guys were not nice to anybody, and they were the same ones who were making fun of Virgil's earlier failure. Their names were Giro and Grob, and they were just as stupid as their names were. Arael narrowed his eyes skeptically and then suddenly got a quick vision. In the vision, there was a fight going on, but that was all he saw before it ended.

Arael took immediate action and stood up. "I think Virgil needs help," he said to Orias.

Orias looked at him and then got up too, bringing Nerida with him, he was done eating anyway. The two went off to where Arael had seen Virgil, Giro and Grob go, leaving Ego behind. Once they were out in the hallway, it was quiet. They walked silently and listened for any sounds of a fight. There was no sign of Virgil or anybody else.

"Where'd they go?" Orias asked.

Arael paused for a moment, and then heard voices down the next hall ahead of them. Arael pointed to the hall and then they ran and peeked inside. The boys were out of sight, but they could see their shadows at the end of the hall, and they could hear them talking.

"Come on you scrawny swamp rat, hit me. If you're so tough, hit me," they heard Grob say.

Orias and Arael looked at each other in concern and then went further into the hall.

"What, you're not going to talk? Are you scared?" Giro asked in a mocking tone.

"He didn't do it the last time. He's too chicken. Aye, daddy's boy? Teacher's pet?" Somebody else said.

Suddenly there was the sound of a scuffle, which caused Orias and Arael to run around the corner to see what was going on.

"Stop!" Arael said; though, nobody heard him.

They saw Giro standing in front of Grob and to their surprise, Schlimm too, as the two held Virgil's arms.

"C'mon, Giro, beat some sense into him!" Schlimm laughed.

Giro swung his fat fist into Virgil's face and then proceeded to punch him again and again. Virgil wasn't fighting back for some reason, it didn't make any sense! He could take those guys easily.

"Hey, stop!" Arael yelled again, while Orias's dragon screeched.

This time the bullies heard him and stopped what they were doing, turning their attention to Arael and Orias.

"Hey! Arael, Orias!" Schlimm said happily, leaving Grob to hold onto Virgil as he approached them. "You're just in time, come on, have a whack at him!"

"What!? No! Let him go!" Arael said.

"I thought you were nice, Schlimm!" Orias said in disappointment.

Schlimm looked at them in confusion, like it was them that did something wrong. "I am nice!" He said. "You hate this guy too, don't you? You said it yourself, Arael."

Arael looked at Virgil as he looked back at him. He could see the feeling of sadness in his eyes, even though his face remained emotionless. Arael shook his head no and then Schlimm suddenly grabbed his arm and yanked him toward Virgil.

"Go ahead, give him your best shot, it'll make you feel better," Schlimm said. "I should've asked you the last few times, but you were busy."

"No!" Arael said.

"The last few times? You've been bullying him under our noses?" Orias asked with a shaky tone; what he really wanted to do was run away, but he couldn't do that to Arael and Virgil.

"Yeah, what're you going to do about it, runt?" Giro asked with a smirk.

"Now, now. Don't talk that way to Orias," Schlimm said.

Orias just stood there, he didn't know what to do in these situations. Nerida spoke for him by screeching angrily and raising her wings to look scary, but the bullies only laughed at her.

"Grob, just let him go, it's not worth it," Arael said.

Grob smiled at Arael like an idiot and refused to let go of Virgil.

"Come on, buddy, go ahead, hit him," Schlimm said, nudging Arael closer.

Arael would've wanted to hit Virgil before, but now he knew that he was being stupid, and he felt horrible about it. Virgil didn't do anything wrong. He was always watching everyone's backs. Now he was mad at Schlimm. Schlimm was the person that he should've been angry with all along, including himself.

"Yeah, Schlimm, I'll hit somebody, but it's not going to be Virgil!" Arael said, turning to Schlimm. "Tell Grob to let go of him!"

Schlimm looked hurt by Arael's words. "What? I thought we were friends!"

"I'm serious!" Arael yelled. He was annoyed that they weren't listening to him.

"Arael, it's okay, I can take care of it," Virgil finally said.

Just then, Schlimm turned around and punched Virgil in the stomach to shut him up. "Like the last time? You sure handled that well, freak boy!" He laughed.

Suddenly, Arael grabbed Schlimm by the shirt and yanked him back, before punching him in the chin. Arael was just the right height to hit the taller boy precise enough to knock him down. Schlimm looked dumbfounded when his butt met the ground.

"Kick their cheeks!" Schlimm ordered the other brick heads.

Grob pushed Virgil to the ground and went after Arael and Orias with Giro. Orias backed up in fear when Giro came after him, and then Nerida suddenly leapt up and bit Giro's nose, causing him to panic and spin around. When Grob came after Arael, Arael tried to punch him, but it didn't do much to the blubbery teen. Giro laughed and lunged to grab Arael, but he was able dodge him.

"Hey!" They heard. Everyone paused and turned to see Ego standing down the hall before them. "You've got three seconds before I beat you to a pulp!" She growled.

Giro and Grob looked at Schlimm, waiting for him to make a decision for them. Schlimm stood up and looked to Ego as she cracked her knuckles. Ego had beaten them up before, and it didn't end well. Giro was actually the red headed kid that Ego had beaten up on their first day, so he didn't want to stick around to see what would happen next. Besides, they were outnumbered now, Ego counting as two.

Schlimm backed up and ran away, followed by his goons. Giro tripped and scrambled after the other two, calling for them to wait up before finally getting back to his feet. Ego crossed her arms and huffed, and then she and Arael went to try and help Virgil. Orias picked Nerida up off of the ground after she'd fallen off of Giro's nose. Arael held his hand out to Virgil, but he refused it and got up on his own. He looked in the direction that the bullies had gone and then looked at the floor with a bloody and frustrated face.

"Are you okay?" Ego asked, raising an eyebrow at him.

"I've been better... Worse too..." Virgil sighed.

"Why didn't you fight back? You could beat them easily, couldn't you?" Arael asked.

"Oh, believe me, I could beat those fools with a flick of my wrist..." Virgil said in annoyance. "But... I refuse to hurt people unless I have to."

"But you did have to! They were beating you up!" Arael said.

Virgil shrugged, "Stuff happens. Thanks for the help..." Virgil looked at Arael like he'd forgotten that Schlimm said that Arael hated him.

Arael just stared at him in confusion. Everything that Virgil did or said didn't make any sense to him. "Is that what happened to your cheek that one time in the washroom? They beat you up?" Arael asked.

Virgil nodded yes in reply. "Don't tell anybody..."

"Why not?" Ego asked. "They could get punished badly, so they'd have to leave you alone for good."

"Just don't. It's not worth it. They're stupid anyway," Virgil said. "It's not like my dad didn't do it every day..." He mumbled under his breath.

Quickly, Arael got a vision of the Pneumati and the face of a man with glowing eyes, and a pool of white liquid behind him. The same voice as when Arael was in the washroom screamed, "You have to trust me!" Once the vision had ended, Arael blinked and looked up at Virgil, a bit dazed. Everybody must've noticed his change in behavior because they were all staring at him.

"Did you just get one of those Dreamwalker visions?" Orias asked.

"Yeah..." Arael answered, still looking at Virgil. "How come I always get these visions when you're around, Virgil?" Virgil stared at him, having nothing to say about it. "Do you have nightmares about the Pneumati?" Arael asked.

Virgil looked at the floor for a moment, and then back to Arael. "Every single night... You think you're getting into my head?" Virgil almost looked worried, like he didn't want Arael to see his dreams.

"Maybe," Arael said. "I'm going to talk to Chancellor Hofmeister about it..."

"You've had bad experiences with the Pneumati too, eh?" Ego asked.

"Worse than you could ever imagine," Virgil said, brushing his hair back, they'd almost forgotten that one of his eyes was messed up. "I need to lie down..."

Arael nodded as Virgil waved and then went off to go to his room. Arael really wanted to know what Virgil's experiences with the Pneumati were now. It was probably insensitive to ask though... Arael wouldn't want to reflect on his own bad experiences, even though he really didn't have many yet. He was lucky that his father protected him while giving him the best life that he could. The only horrible experience Arael could remember was when his mother had died, and the few years after that. He didn't talk about that much. His father didn't either. They weren't good memories...

CHAPTER SIXTEEN

Visions

"Every time Virgil is around? That's very interesting," said the Chancellor, as she put books away on shelves around her chamber.

Arael was following her, telling her about all of his visions and what he suspected was causing them. "He said he'd been having nightmares about the Pneumati, so I think I might be getting glimpses of those," he said, "But I don't know what it has to do with anything!"

The Chancellor let go of a book and allowed it to levitate up to an empty spot on a high shelf. "Perhaps you have a connection with him," she suggested.

Arael stopped and thought about it for a moment and then started pacing around the room. "Why would I? I haven't liked him very much up until now. I still don't like him very much..."

"Or he to you…" the Chancellor added. "Have you heard any voices in them?"

Arael spun around on his heels. "Yes! I have!" He answered. "There's this familiar voice, but I can't figure out who it is. I think it's a boy, but it could be a girl just as easily. The first time it said something like, 'Arael, please help me you need to have trust in me!' and the second time it said pretty much the same thing, 'You have to trust me!'"

"Whose voice to you think it is?" The Chancellor asked.

Arael sat down on a little red cushion and put his face in his hands for a moment, grumbling as he thought about who the voice might've been. He couldn't come up with any good answers. It was annoying because the answer was right there, like he could've said it right then, but it just wasn't registering in his brain.

"Well, it's obviously somebody that I don't trust."

He picked up his journal off of a side table and started flipping through the pages that were filled with things from his visions.

"Do you trust Orias?" The Chancellor asked.

Arael nodded yes.

"Ego?"

He nodded yes again.

"Virgil?"

"Yeah, I trust him… He's never done anything to me. I'm just a jerk…" Arael huffed. "There are a ton of people that I don't trust, but they don't sound even close to the same as that voice!"

"It will come to you. Dreamwalkers have to be patient with their abilities. They may not make sense at first, but they will when the time comes," the Chancellor smiled.

"I guess…" Arael sighed. "I'm not that great at being patient."

The Chancellor laughed and then patted Arael's shoulder. "My husband was never very patient about it either," she said. "You're a lot like he was when he was young."

Arael looked at the Chancellor in confusion. "Your husband was a Dreamwalker?" He asked. "I didn't even know you had a husband."

"Indeed. But his ability doesn't work well anymore."

"It wears off?" Arael asked in concern.

"No, he was injured and it became painful for him so I had to suppress it with my magic."

"Is he dead?"

"Oh, no, no, he's just fine," the Chancellor giggled.

Just then, Sir Enzo walked into the room in full armor. He wasn't paying attention to what he was doing and accidentally knocked over a vase before catching it and putting it back. He spoke as he tromped into the room, looking at a scroll in his hand, "Milady, the messenger brought a scroll with recent Pneumati activities written down on it. I'm afraid we're going to have to take care of them again before they get too close. I'm leaving the watchmen on high alert until I get ba—" before Enzo finished, he finally looked up and noticed that Arael was standing in the room. "Oh! Good day, Arael!"

"Uh… Good day," Arael said.

The Chancellor put all of her things down and went to Enzo. "Where have they been spotted?" She asked.

"Near the perimeter of Tarragon," Enzo answered. "They're getting restless now that we have all of the younglings... I fear they'll stop at nothing to find them."

The Chancellor nodded, concerned about what the Pneumati were doing as well. "Alright, be cautious."

Enzo nodded in reply as the Chancellor gave him a quick hug, and then he turned to leave.

"Sir Enzo, wait!" Arael said. "Can I come with you!?"

Enzo stopped and looked at Arael. "You're not a knight yet."

"But I have my sword, I've trained! You've seen me! I want to help!" Arael insisted.

"Another day, boy," Enzo smiled, before leaving.

Arael stared at the door after Enzo left, and then looked at the Chancellor. "Another day? Did that mean something?" He asked, trying to get anything out of context that he could.

"He's quite confident in you," said the Chancellor. "Is there anything more that you wish to speak of?"

Arael thought about it for a moment and then shook his head no. He was sure that he'd told her everything about his visions. He even told her about the dreams that he had in the time just before he came to Mountainglaive... He wanted to try and decode them more, but the Chancellor had some work to do now, and he understood that, so he went on his way.

It was getting dark as the day was ending, and it was storming outside. The hallways were mostly empty because the students had gone to bed once again. Arael's brain was still going on and on about his visions, so he decided to go up into one of the watch towers. From there, he could see Enzo and some of the other knights as they got on their horses and left the castle. He could see part of Tarragon as well, down passed all of the jagged rocks, through the woods and across a river. It still looked as amazing as it did when he first saw it.

Arael leaned over the barrier of the watch tower to see the land below. It was beginning to get chilly outside, since winter was coming. The wind sprayed the sleet into Arael's face, but it felt nice. The watch tower was a good place to be alone with one's thoughts. Arael had seen some of the other students studying, or reading books up there before, including Virgil.

Arael sighed as the sleet became more aggressive, drowning out all other noises. He ran his fingers over a shield decoration that was carved into the stone barrier, and then looked down at the red decorations on his uniform. He had yet to meet his legion master, Ariese. If he even existed... Every time he saw the symbol on his chest, it made him want to be a knight more. Arael took one more look at the terrain below and then retired to his room for the rest of the night.

CHAPTER SEVENTEEN
Tests

The next morning, when the children had gone to Enzo's field training class, they waited for him to return, but he never did. They were worried that their most beloved mentor would never return, but they knew that sometimes it took a while for the knights to come back from battle. They waited the entire class period, without a sign of Enzo, so they went on to their next classes. This went on for about three days, until Sir Enzo finally showed up to supper. The students were all happy to see him, and he was happy to see them in turn, but he had some bad news for the Chancellor. They didn't know what the bad news was, but by the look of Enzo's face, it definitely was something they had to worry about.

Over the next few days, Enzo seemed to be quite exhausted and distant during class. The students tried asking him what was going on, but he always smiled and insisted that there was nothing for them to worry about.

The Watchmen were on guard more than usual, they were actually living statues, who acted as tower defense. Orias always tried to talk to the Watchmen, like everything else, but it just made him look crazy. The Watchmen moved about, nobody ever saw them do it, but now most of them were staying in their places, permanently on guard.

The kids were finally getting to some interesting things in their classes now. They were learning more real world skills from Enzo that could save lives; they were also learning common spells in Lady Agnes's class. Sir Gwenael and Lady Ida were showing them the basics on making their own armor. Only the students that became knights or true blacksmiths were going to make armor, but it was good for everyone to learn. The true blacksmiths would do this for a living someday... Even Sir Adonis was teaching something different; he was still a jerk, but they were actually learning some things from him for once, like fighting techniques. Sir Adonis must've finally noticed that they weren't getting anywhere with what he was doing before.

It was snowing on this particular day, but they were out in the field again anyway, at the beginning of Enzo's class. This time they had their second draft weapons with them, and were going to try something different. All of the students stood in a line as usual, while Enzo paced in front of them, stroking his mustache.

"So... Younglings, I haven't been completely honest with you," Enzo started. They looked at him in confusion, because Enzo was always honest with them, but they were sure that they knew what this was about. He still hadn't told them what had happened with the Pneumati. "The Pneumati are looking for us. They're searching every nook and cranny to find our location... So we have limited time with your training now..." Enzo continued. "I'm very impressed with you all, for you have been doing quite well with all that we've been throwing at you. So, that being said, the Chancellor, and the legion masters have set a date for when you will be chosen for the legions."

The students looked at each other and cheered in excitement. This is what they'd been waiting for this whole time! Arael and Orias were probably the most excited out of everyone. They were eager to know more about the legions, and who would be chosen.

Enzo silenced them, so that he could continue to explain things. "You all have to pass a series of tests that each of your mentors have set up for you, which will increase your chances of becoming knights in your own legions. I already have my test set up. I'm going to put you through it twice, once today, and the second test will be after all of your other tests are completed," he explained. "Now... Whoever is going to be in the legions, will be decided in nine days..."

Nine days!? That wasn't a lot of time to do all of these tests! This meant that the Pneumati must've really been closing in! They were still excited about the possibility of being chosen for the legions, but they felt overwhelmed too. They would be doing a test each day, until the ninth day, which would be the time of the legion ceremony. This would be hard, but if they were to be real knights in these legions, they had to be strong. The tests were probably going to be physically and mentally exhausting.

Enzo stood in front of them, with his hands behind his back. "I told you that this class wouldn't be tough until you became serious knights... Well... Now you're in the beginning steps of becoming just that. I may end up losing the title of 'favorite mentor' soon enough," he smiled. "Now for the first test... We're going to play a survival game." Enzo's tone changed; it was a little bit unsettling, but they knew that he was being serious now. "You're going to enter the arch again. Once inside the arch, you will be placed in a random area of the Grimwood Forest. You can either be a lone wolf out there, or you can team up with others. You will use everything that you have learned to your advantage, even your weapons. This will test your strength and bravery, to see how you really preform under pressure. None of you will die. None of you will be injured long term. The arch's magic won't allow it. But if you are struck down, then you are out of the game. Students who last until the clock strikes midnight will pass the test. The first time is just luck, but the next time, we'll know if you're really ready. Understood?"

Arael and Orias stared at Enzo in surprise. Midnight? That would be fifteen hours from now! They were not expecting this from Enzo at all. There had to be some secret to passing this test. Arael was worried about Orias. He still wasn't very good at much. He had lord Zander's ax now, but he couldn't use it well. Arael could tell that Orias was worried too. At least he had Nerida with him, and she had that pendant around her neck, which increased luck slightly. She counted as one of Orias's weapons.

"Now, get in there," Enzo said, pointing to the magic arch.

Some of the students decided to dash straight into the arch with no thought, others hesitated, still feeling overwhelmed. Arael and Orias stood still for a moment, staring at the arch.

"I'm scared, Arael!" Orias said, grabbing Arael's surcoat.

"It's going to be okay, I'll find you," Arael said. "You can do this!"

Just then, Arael dashed off into the arch, leaving Orias behind.

"Arael! Arael! Wait!" Orias cried, deciding to run after him.

That was the only way to get him in there... After Areal had gone into the arch, he appeared in the Grimwood Forest, just as Enzo said he would. There was a lot more snow and the forest was dark and creepy; that was the reason it was called the Grimwood Forest. The trees looked like they could come to life and chase you... This forest was magic, and it really didn't even exist in

the real world. It was a place that only magic entrances –
like the arch – could take someone to.

Arael was all alone and it was deathly quiet. He
gripped the hilt of his sword, making him feel a bit safer
in the moment. He could see his breath floating in front
of his face every time he exhaled... Now he had to find
Orias... Arael started walking, his boots crunched in the
icy snow with every step. There wasn't much to see out
there besides trees and snow. It looked like a black and
white portrait.

He suddenly heard a girl's scream, causing him to
whirl around trying to make out where it was coming
from. Next, he heard some voices, belonging to too
many people for him to take on his own, so he ran.
Branches hit his face and caught the fabric of his clothes
as he ran. Arael kept going until he couldn't run
anymore, stopping at a clearing in the trees. He realized
that he was actually scared... He didn't want the other
kids to catch and 'kill' him. It used to be all fun and
games, but reality was starting to set in now. Arael was
by himself, and had to put his skills to the test; he had to
survive in a test that was the closest thing to reality that
he was going to get until he was a true knight.

Arael heard a twig snap behind him, and quickly drew
his sword as he spun around to see what was there. There
was only a bird. Arael scanned the area and kept his
sword ready, gripping it firmly with his gloved hands.
He paused for a moment and took a long breath to ease
himself.

"Come on... I can do this. I'm braver than this," he told himself.

He stood up straight and calmed down enough to look at his surroundings efficiently. He could hear the sound of a river nearby... Rivers were good, weren't they? He could follow the river and find a place to hide. He could drink from it if the water was acceptable... The only problem was that other kids might have the same idea. Arael wanted to avoid the others, but the river might have been his best option; if Orias payed attention to anything that he'd been taught, then maybe Arael could find him there too. Besides, if Arael ran into anybody, he could take them. He was one of the top fighters in combat class... Well, at least he thought. That's what Sir Cornelius told him before he died. Arael was able to hold his ground for a good amount of time against Sir Adonis too, and if he could do that, then he could beat most of the kids in Mountainglaive.

Arael decided to quit wasting time thinking about it, and headed off toward the river. When he arrived, it was much larger than he thought it would be. It had to have been at least thirty meters across. The water was cold too. If somebody fell in there, they'd certainly be out of the game. Arael looked up the river and decided to travel that way, against the flow. He heard somebody else scream in the distance, but it wasn't close enough for him to be worried. Somebody must have already formed a group and was going after the weaker kids, or somebody was just picking them off all alone. It could've been Ego; she seemed like the kind of person that would do something like that. Luckily, Schlimm wasn't in this class. Giro and Grob weren't either, but even if they were, they had no skills whatsoever. Those two would just end up wandering off of a cliff and then wonder what went wrong.

Arael kept walking, watching the ground as he went. There were a lot of things hidden under the snow that he had to watch out for. He hadn't seen anybody yet, but he was expecting to at any moment. He could see where the sun was, and by the looks of it, it had only been about an hour since he'd entered the arch. He wondered if Orias was doing okay, if he was still in the game at all… Arael thought about looking for Virgil. Virgil was smart, he'd know what to do, and he was probably around the river somewhere too. Arael was afraid that Virgil might try to strike him down though. If that happened, then there was no way that Arael would be able to fight him. Then again, Virgil did say that he 'doesn't hurt people unless he has to.' Arael didn't know the extent of what that meant… If the arch didn't allow anybody to get hurt, then Virgil could've been dropping them like flies out there.

A wolf howled nearby, like the ghost of the forest that it was. That was another thing that Arael had to look out for, wild animals. Those were the least of his concerns though. Arael looked up ahead, finally breaking his gaze from the ground and immediately spotted some kids. Startled, he jumped behind a tree and peeked around it to get a better look of who he'd seen. Luckily, they were looking away from him and didn't notice his presence.

There were three of them standing near the river. Arael didn't know who they were, but he didn't want to go out there to ask.

The kids were laughing as one of them stood with his feet in the river. It looked like they had just finished pushing somebody in. Whoever they pushed in was gone now. It was a spell that was called 'Defugio' that enabled the arch to magically transport people from one place to another. Arael learned that a few days ago. It was a more advanced spell that the mages would get to learn sooner or later.

The three kids finally stepped away from the water and continued on, coming closer to Arael's hiding place. Arael wasn't worried that they would see him, he was good at hiding. After all of those years that he'd spent hiding from the Pneumati, it became a useful skill. He couldn't run fast though. Anybody could catch him if he was being chased... Arael watched as they passed him by and then he took a long breath of relief.

He went to step out of hiding and continue up the river once they were gone, but unexpectedly, he felt a cold metal blade against his throat, while another hand held onto the back of his surcoat. Arael gasped in surprise. How could he have not heard this person sneaking up behind him!? Now he was going to fail the test! There was no way it was going to be that easy to take him down! He'd put his sword back into its scabbard earlier, so there was no way he could get to it before his head was sliced off now!

Arael stared at the tree in front of him with wide eyes, while his mouth hung open in a silent scream. His attacker hadn't done anything yet... Instead he saw the attacker's face peek at him from over his shoulder. Arael shifted his eyes to see who it was, and wasn't sure if he was relieved or even more terrified when he realized who it was. Virgil... Who else would've been able to sneak up behind him without a sound? Virgil smiled at him and then slowly removed the knife from Arael's flesh. Virgil put his finger to his lips, telling Arael to hush, and then pointed up to the tree. Virgil kept his grip on Arael as they both looked up. There was a girl on a branch, right above them. Arael didn't even notice her before.

The girl had a bow and arrows, and she was aiming at the three kids that were walking down the river. Arael and Virgil waited until she let her arrow lose, hitting one of the kids. It was a great shot, and it struck him out of the game. The other two looked around in panic and then the girl let another arrow fly, hitting the next kid. The third looked up and figured out where the arrows were coming from, so he drew his sword and decided to come after the girl.

Arael tried to pull away from Virgil to run, since the boy was coming toward them now, but Virgil wouldn't let him go. The boy stopped in front of the tree and started yelling at the girl as she readied another arrow. The boy taunted her into carelessly shooting at him, and then he deflected the arrow with his sword, but suddenly, she shot another one and hit him while he was distracted;

at the same time, the girl slipped and fell backwards out of the tree. Now both of them were out of the game.

"Stuff happens," Virgil said, winking at Arael before letting go of him.

Arael's heart was pounding in his chest. He felt like he couldn't breathe, and he was angry with Virgil for holding him in place. Arael suddenly felt panicked, expecting Virgil to strike him down, so he quickly grabbed his sword and swung it at full force as he spun around on his heels. Arael yelled loudly with his swinging force, hitting nothing. He clenched his teeth in a mixture of panic and anger as his breath puffed from his mouth into white clouds. To his surprise, there was nobody there. Virgil was gone. He'd left him just like that... Now Arael was mad that Virgil left him! If he wasn't going to strike him out of the game, then he could've at least stuck around to help out! Virgil didn't even leave any noticeable footprints behind!

Arael tossed his sword on the ground and growled loudly as he gripped at his hair. Now he was beginning to confuse himself with all of these mixed feelings... He paused for a moment to calm down a little bit, picking up his sword and putting it back into its scabbard.

"This is absolute nonsense!" He said.

Another thing he would've liked to know was where on Domhan Virgil got a knife. The kids had only been able to have one weapon on them that he knew of. Maybe Virgil was a cheater all this time and that's why he'd been so good at everything. Arael's thoughts were interrupted by another wolf howling. This time it was much closer. Arael stepped out from behind the trees and glanced up the river, where there was a rocky area ahead. He scanned the rocks for a moment and then caught a flash of a familiar figure, moving through the trees near the rocky area on the other side of the river.

"Orias?" Arael said. Arael ran toward the rocks and climbed up, to see if he could get a better look at the other side of the river. The rocks were icy and slippery, so he had to be careful. "Orias!" Arael called out.

The wolf howled again, the noise coming from the same place that he saw Orias. Arael hoped that it hadn't gotten his friend. He waited there for a moment, staring at the woods, and then saw a flash of blue and brown again. This time, it was coming toward the river. As it came closer, Arael could see the black uniform and the blue decorations on it that belonged to Orias.

"Hey! Orias!" Arael called, waving at him.

"Arael!?" Orias yelled, out of breath.

As Orias came closer, Arael could see that he was running. He watched as Orias quickly climbed up some of the rocks near the river and tried to run across them. The rocks were too slippery, causing Orias to lose his footing and fall. Nerida ran to his side, and pulled on his surcoat to try and help him up. Arael saw something else too. It was a grey wolf.

"Orias! Watch out! Run!" Arael yelled, scared for Orias.

The wolf ran up to Orias and then stopped in front of him, when an even bigger wolf jumped out of the woods. There was a kid sitting on the larger wolf's back. That kid must've been one of the direwolf riders! The grey wolf growled at the direwolf and then suddenly attacked it! The grey wolf seemed to be protecting Orias! Arael was shocked.

"Come on Orias! Come on!" Arael yelled, waving at his friend.

There were rocks that Orias could jump onto that led to Arael's side of the river, but it wasn't going to be easy to navigate them. Orias scrambled to his feet as the grey wolf and the direwolf fought each other, and then he hopped onto the first rock. Arael kept on calling for him as he leaped to the next rock and then the next. Orias slipped a few times, but he eventually got to Arael. Arael caught him before he slipped into the water, and then pulled him back. They stopped and watched as the wolves continued to fight, until the kid eventually tumbled off of the direwolf's back and got stepped on, which caused both of them to disappear. Once the kid and the direwolf were gone, the grey wolf stopped and looked at Arael and Orias, before howling and disappearing into the forest.

"I'm so glad you're still here!" Arael said, hugging his friend. "How'd you get that wolf to help you!?"

Orias pushed Arael away, trying to catch his breath, and then he picked up Nerida from the ground. "He was helping me this whole time," he answered. "I guess I can get other animals to help me! I'm glad you're still here too! I was worried I'd never find you!"

Arael looked around for a moment and then checked the sun again. "Come on, we probably attracted attention with all of that noise. We should find a place to wait this out."

"Oh! I saw a cave up the river, not too far from here. It was out of the way enough for us to be okay there," Orias said.

Arael nodded and then they headed off toward the cave that Orias had seen. Once they found the cave, they inspected it and then built a small fire near the opening so that they could keep warm. Orias had lost a glove somewhere in the woods, so his hand was freezing cold. They were able to stay there for a long time, and they were comfortable with staying until the test ended. Activity was stirring up more and more outside as the hours went on. There was a quick wind storm that took down a few trees, and there was some kind of animal rampage that they'd heard going on somewhere.

Arael peeked at the sky, from the cave opening. It was dark now, and by the looks of it, they had at least three hours left in the game. The wind was blowing loudly, making it hard to hear. They needed to stay extra alert now, because they had a feeling the worst was about to come, and it was getting colder out.

Orias was beginning to get tired, so Arael let him sleep while he kept watch. Arael was getting tired too, as he sat still, staring at the ground in front of himself. He held his sword in his hands, just in case he had to use it. He listened to the wind howling, as a few tree branches snapped off and fell to the ground nearby. Behind Arael, Orias and Nerida were sleeping, but something else woke up.

From a small crack in the wall of the cave, a strange, feathery snake peeked out. The snake slithered down the wall, to the ground near the sleeping boy and over the small dragon's tail. This woke Nerida up and then she turned around to see what it was. When she saw the snake, she screeched and hopped around, getting Arael's attention and waking Orias up.

"What!? What is it?" Arael asked.

Orias looked at Nerida and then saw the snake crawling on him. "Snake!" He yelled.

Arael saw the snake as soon as Orias announced it. This wasn't just any snake. It was the extremely venomous Shrikey snake. Arael had forgotten that they liked to come out at night, even in cold weather because of their feathers. Before Arael could warn Orias of what it was, Orias's movements startled the snake, causing it to stand up and flash a bright hood of white and teal feathers at him before striking his hand. Orias jumped up and shook the snake off, letting Nerida kill it.

"Orias!?" Arael said in concern.

Orias looked at Arael and tried to speak, before he quickly fell over, disappearing with Nerida... Orias was out of the game now... Killed by a snake...

"No!" Arael yelled.

He looked at the dead snake and then backed away from it. If there was one snake here, then there were going to be more. As if on que, three more snakes started to emerge from cracks in the walls of the cave, whistling as their tongues flapped. Arael immediately grabbed his sword from the ground and dashed from the cave. He had to be careful where he stepped, because the Shrikey snakes could've been hiding in the snow too. Now he didn't have a hiding place, and he was alone again… The forest seemed much more alive than it was before. There were noises coming from the trees and some kind of creature's cackle was sounding from all directions. It was hair-raising. Arael continued through the woods, forgetting about the river. The river was just going to be another obstacle now that it was pitch dark, especially with the slippery rocks around it. The last thing that he needed was an accident to take him out.

As Arael traveled through the forest, he began to feel like he wasn't alone. Every time he heard a twig snap, or snow crunching, he whirled around to see what it was. His back tensed up, feeling the presence of somebody behind him, even though there was nothing there when he looked. The feeling was getting more and more intense as the time came down to ten thirty. Arael paused when he heard another twig snap, this time it was louder than the rest. He was getting tired of the feeling of being followed.

"Hey! I know you're there, so quit following me!" He yelled out, to make sure whoever was out there could hear him.

He waited for a response, and then he suddenly felt the presence disappear… What he said must have worked… Just then, Arael heard a loud, haunting scream. It was way too close for comfort. The scream startled him enough to send him running through the forest. Arael caught a glimpse of a shadow figure from the corner of his eye and quickly whipped his head around to see it. He came to a stop and stared at whatever was standing there. It was hard to see in the dark. The figure caused Arael to get a sense of serious déjà vu, but he didn't know why. Arael shifted his position to see the figure better, but then it was gone, so he started running again. The feeling of being followed was back, but now he felt like he was being chased.

Arael kept running, until he reached a large rock with a pile of dead leaves next to it. Arael looked closer at the pile of leaves and then finally remembered where this was from. The dream that he had just before he left Breckenridge... Arael knew what happened in the dream when he saw the pile of leaves... There was something dead lying there, causing Arael to fear the worst, but when he got closer, it wasn't who he thought it would be. It was one of the kids from his class. The kid disappeared in front of him. Arael was afraid to find out how he was struck down. It had to have been only seconds before he'd arrived.

Arael knew what was going to happen next if that dream was the same as this situation. Abruptly, he heard something behind him and he quickly turned around, expecting the terrible Pneumati figure to be standing there. He was ready to fight, but he ended up tripping on a log and falling backwards.

"Get away!" Arael yelled, just like in his dream.

There was indeed a figure in front of him, and he couldn't see it well in the dark until it came closer and stopped above him to stare. The figure suddenly lunged toward him, and that was as far as his dream went before...

To Arael's surprise, he was yanked to his feet, and then he heard a familiar voice, "Illustro." A bright ball of light appeared and lit up everything around them. Virgil had found him once again. This time, Arael was definitely happy to see him.

"Virgil, it's you!" Arael said in relief.

"Yes, it's me!" Virgil said, grabbing Arael's arm. "Come on, we have to get out of here now!"

Virgil put his light out and started leading him through the forest. Arael stayed with Virgil until they got to an old, stone tower that was mostly buried under the dirt and snow. It was an acceptable hiding place for the time being. Virgil took Arael behind the stone tower so they could catch their breath.

"What's chasing us?" Arael asked.

Arael could see that Virgil looked afraid, which made him feel even more panicked. It was always weird to see a new expression on his face. Virgil continuously glanced around, looking for whatever was following them. He was either avoiding Arael's question, or he didn't hear him.

"Virgil!" Arael said, getting his attention. "What is chasing us?"

"Pneumati," Virgil answered.

Arael's eyes widened in terror. He had a feeling that it was the Pneumati that were after them, but now that he heard it spoken aloud, it sent chills down his spine.

All of a sudden, Arael got a vision through someone else's eyes, it was brief, but it showed him enough. When the vision was done, Arael looked and saw a shadow figure, standing exactly where he thought it would be. It didn't quite look the same as the Pneumati he'd seen before. Maybe because it wasn't a real one... Either way, it was terrifying.

"Virgil! Look out!" Arael said.

Virgil turned toward the Pneumati just as it jumped for them, and then he yelled out a spell almost too late, "Aegis!" throwing his arms up in defense. A barrier of bright green light suddenly appeared, hitting the Pneumati and causing it to screech like an animal. The barrier quickly disappeared after making contact with the Pneumati, turning the vile creature to dust.

Arael and Virgil didn't stick around to see what would happen next. They ran from their hiding place and dashed through the woods. They had no idea where they were going now, and they knew that if there was one Pneumati, then there had to be more. Pneumati never traveled alone, even if this wasn't real. Arael was having trouble keeping up with Virgil. He couldn't run well at all, while Virgil could've won any race. He watched as Virgil got too far ahead of him, and then he saw a Pneumati leap from the trees and take Virgil down.

"Virgil!" Arael yelled, drawing his sword as he tried to catch up to them.

Virgil panicked as the Pneumati attacked him, he wasn't thinking straight anymore. Normally he would've known exactly what to do, but now he was acting like a helpless child. Arael sprinted up behind the Pneumati, swinging his sword at it. The sword stuck into the creature's side, knocking it off of Virgil. Virgil rolled up to his feet and spun his swallow wand around once, smashing the end of it into the head of a Pneumati that had just appeared behind Arael. Virgil had the Aegis crystal that he'd found during the treasure hunt in the blunt end of his wand, so the crystal burned the Pneumati after he hit it.

The Aegis crystal burned the Pneumati so badly that when Arael turned around, he could see a skull. He didn't expect the Pneumati to actually be flesh and blood, he thought that they were ghosts. The Pneumati growled at Virgil and shot a blast of dark magic his way. The magic gave Arael a horrible sick feeling as soon as it manifested. The magic hit Virgil in the arm when he tried to dodge it, causing him to let out a terrible shriek and drop his weapon. The magic burned his sleeve off and was eating away at his arm. His arm looked black, and blood dripped into the white snow.

Arael gasped, he thought that the arch didn't let them get hurt! While the Pneumati's back was turned to Arael, he struck it down before it could do any more damage. Once the Pneumati was dead, Arael went to grab Virgil to help him up.

"Don't touch my arm!" Virgil warned. "It spreads!"

Arael looked at Virgil's arm and then went to his other side and got him to his feet.

"Use healing magic!" Arael said.

"I can't!"

"You're a mage aren't you!? Mages can use healing magic!"

"Arael, I don't know how!" Virgil admitted.

Virgil picked up his swallow wand and then they started to run again. Arael didn't know how they were supposed to get away from the Pneumati. All that he ever did was hide from them. As they were running, Arael glanced around, spotting more Pneumati manifesting around them. It looked like there was going to be no way out. Arael didn't want to lose this! He couldn't believe this was happening! They'd come too far for it to end like this! He looked at Virgil's arm and cringed at the blackened skin as it began to spread like fire. The black magic slowly destroyed you from the inside out. Arael knew that it was painful.

Pneumati suddenly blocked their path. Arael and Virgil looked around, finding no way out. It was like a terrible nightmare! Arael's heart felt like it was jumping straight out of his chest and back in through his throat! The two stood back to back as the creatures closed in on them.

"Use Aegis!" Arael yelled.

Virgil heard him, but he stuttered when he tried to cast Aegis. Virgil didn't seem so invincible now... One of the Pneumati jumped toward Arael, but he was able to slice its head off.

"Aegis, Virgil! Aegis, now!" Arael roared.

Virgil finally snapped out of it and then did what Arael wanted, "Aegi-" before he could finish, one of the Pneumati in front of Arael shot a concentrated rod of black magic at them. Arael tried to block it, but the rod went straight through his chest and then out through Virgil. They were both dumbfounded, and it felt horribly real! When they knew that they were done for, they saw the Pneumati disappear, and then they fell to the ground.

The next thing Arael knew, he was sitting in the field outside of the magic arch, he gripped at his chest, gasping in panic, and then he realized that he was fine. He looked up and saw all of the other kids in his class, who were standing before him. He turned around and saw that Virgil was curled up on the ground, gripping his ears and panicking. "It never ends, it never ends," he said over and over again.

"Virgil, we're alright!" Arael said.

Virgil didn't stop, so Arael grabbed his wrists and took his hands away from his ears, "Virgil!" He shouted. "It wasn't real!"

Virgil was startled when Arael grabbed his wrists and then tried to pull away, but Arael didn't let go.

"I'm sorry, I'm sorry!" Virgil cried.

Sir Enzo ran up next to them and got down on his knees. He wasn't sure what was going on with the boy, or how to help. Arael let go of Virgil's wrists and then grabbed his face to force him to look at him. Virgil grabbed Arael's arms and closed his eyes tightly like Arael was going to hurt him.

"Virgil, calm down! It's me, Arael! It's over!" Arael said firmly, as he shook Virgil to get his attention.

Virgil opened his eyes and then he stopped panicking. "Arael...?" He squeaked. "I'm sorry... I didn't mean to..."

"What on Domhan is the problem, Virgil? I thought this would be nothing for you!" Orias asked, as he pushed through the crowd.

Arael helped Virgil stand up, he looked ashamed of himself now. "I'm sorry..." Virgil said again.

Sir Enzo stood up and then all of the students looked at him. He crossed his arms and scanned them with his eyes before shaking his head no, more so in concern than anything.

"I must say that I'm a bit disappointed..." Enzo said. "Not a single one of you made it to the end... It's obvious to me that you don't understand what has to be done in these situations. I hope that next time, you'll know. I had some hope for a few of you, but then you crushed it with your reckless decisions."

Everyone stared at Enzo sadly. They were disappointed in themselves now. Arael was sure that he knew what he did wrong... Virgil couldn't let himself be okay with failure, so he was beating himself up inside. Orias was sad, but he really didn't care much. As for Ego, they weren't sure what happened to her, but she was standing there with them. She looked angry as always, but she looked extra angry. She must've made a dumb mistake that led to her downfall.

"Off to bed, all of you. You each have another test to complete tomorrow morning," Enzo said, bringing the class to an end for the day.

All of the students walked off, thinking about what they'd done wrong. They weren't expecting that test to be so difficult. They realized that they were going to have to treat these tests more seriously. Even Virgil mistreated it in some way; he got too cocky at the beginning. They didn't come up with a strategy, and most of them didn't make teams. They all underestimated the work that needed to be done to survive on their own. Most of them were used to being protected by others, instead of taking matters into their own hands.

CHAPTER EIGHTEEN
Serious

Over the next few days, the students took their tests like their lives depended on it; because in reality, their lives really did depend on it. If there was a serious threat out there that they were training to defeat, then every bit of knowledge and skill that they could learn and master was useful. A lot of the kids crumbled under the pressure and failed most of the tests. They even gave up on trying. Arael was surprised at how well Orias was holding up now compared to how Virgil was. It was like the two had switched positions. Arael wasn't so sure what Virgil was worrying about though, because he was passing all of the tests except for the one in Enzo's class. Now they were feeling the pressure of what being knights was really like.

For a big, intimidating guy, Sir Gwenael's test was not what they had expected. Everyone just took the day to finish the armor pieces that they'd been working on, and were given a score on the quality of them. Sir Gwenael was probably the softest on them out of anyone. Lady Ida's test wasn't that bad either. The kids had to answer some questions about weapons and armor. They had to do a few more things to make sure that their new third draft weapons were completely acceptable as well, because those were the weapons that they would use for the rest of the year.

They had a riding test with two mentors whose names were Adam and Felix. Adam and Felix were brothers, and someday Felix would teach Orias how to ride his dragon. Some riders already had full grown direwolves, but the rest of the kids used horses. The riding test was a bit more difficult. They had to go through an obstacle course with their animals, while using their weapons to strike down dummies.

Arael accidentally fell off of his horse once when he reached out too far for the dummy, and Ego couldn't get her horse to walk at all for a little while. Luckily, the horse that Arael always used usually cooperated with him, it was a beautiful white horse named Blur. Orias wished that he could keep the horse that he used, it was a young brown and white horse named Arthur; Orias wanted to keep all of the animals that he met... Virgil's horse was a grumpy black one named Lucca that didn't seem to like him much. It tried to bite him a few times, but it didn't get in the way of his success. Everyone did an acceptable job in that test, especially Orias. Orias passed with flying colors. Arael was proud of his friend. Orias was definitely born to be a rider.

Gaea's ancient text class and the apothecary, Francesco's class both had boring tests, but most of the kids passed. Virgil passed them easily, while Orias and Ego struggled. Arael was surprised when he came up short and failed Gaea's test. During these tests, he finally figured out what his knight class was. He didn't even think about it until then, but he figured that he was a helm because he matched all of a helm's strengths and weaknesses. It made a lot more sense to him as to why he had more patience for fighting rather than ancient texts... Helms were one of the more boring classes, and they were usually the backbone of any team, but Arael could make it work.

Lady Agnes's test was a bit more challenging, but it was interesting. It was definitely built for mages, since it was the magic class. Aegis was the type of spell that could be cast by anyone, but it was difficult to master. What was even more difficult to master was Aegis Armis – a more advanced form of the spell. Something interesting about any form of Aegis spell, was that it was slightly different for each person. It came in different colors, manifestations, and it even made different sounds.

Everyone was sitting in Lady Agnes's classroom as she tested them on their ability to cast Aegis. If they could cast it even slightly, then she considered that to be a success.

"Now," Lady Agnes said, as she stood on a stage in front of the students, who were sitting on wooden seats below. Lady Agnes was a bit of an oddball, most mages were... She spoke almost too fast for them to understand her, and her hair was a mess. "As you know, Aegis is the most important spell that you could learn, because it burns away evil and I mean, literally burns it..." There was a twinkle in her eye when she said the word 'burn...' She passed out some papers for the kids; they'd studied these papers before, but this was to refresh their memory. "I'll start with my mages, since I expect them to already have Aegis mastered. The rest of you, take note of their movements, and even the way in which they utter the word. Learn from their success and learn from their failure."

Lady Agnes pointed to one of the mages in the class. "You first dear," she said.

Arael watched quietly as the mage shyly approached Lady Agnes. Arael was exhausted from all of the testing that had been going on, so he was lazily sketching for most of the class. Everybody was tired. Lady Agnes stood across from the young mage girl and asked if she was ready before she cast a dark magic spell toward her. The spell was mild, but it was prohibited to use in any other situation. Dark magic was not a good thing, according to everyone in Mountainglaive, it was something created by the Pneumati lord. Every type of magic, or spell was an invention, created by different humans or creatures. Every day, a new, more efficient or more powerful spell was created. The girl cast a dark red colored Aegis spell to block the dark magic, but it got through her spell more than it should have, which meant it wasn't the strongest, but it was good enough. Lady Agnes expected more from the mage...

Lady Agnes called the next mage and then Arael turned his attention to one of his books. Arael hadn't been able to cast Aegis yet, so he was stuck with the fact that he was probably going to fail. Arael's mind drifted as he started looking through a book about dark magic that had to do with the class. He didn't think much of it as he read it. He couldn't even read it well, since he failed the ancient text test, but he could read it well enough. There were some things in it that he hadn't noticed the last time that he'd read it.

Arael paused when he read about one spell in particular. The spell was 'Fluttari Motis.' He went over the spell again and again, trying to figure out where he'd heard that before. After going over the spell a few times, he decided to flip the page and read more. Fluttari Motis was apparently used to levitate objects and beings, usually quite forcefully. Arael looked up from the book for a moment and then he remembered where he'd heard it. The night when he and Orias watched Virgil find the ancient book from the treasure hunt... Virgil used that spell to move the bricks.

Virgil's voice uttering that spell echoed through Arael's head, but then he shook it off and figured that it was just a misunderstanding, so he flipped the pages of the book to find something else. Arael was shocked when he looked at the next page that he fell upon. Sure enough, there was another spell in there that Virgil had used, Infra Therma. That was the spell that he used to freeze the water in the washroom, while they were being attacked by that unknown being.

Arael was confused at why Virgil had used them. Was Virgil even aware that he was using dark magic? Arael's thoughts were suddenly interrupted by a tap on his shoulder, causing him to slam the book shut before looking to see Virgil there. He had forgotten that he was sitting behind him the whole time. He hoped that he didn't see what he was reading.

Virgil held something up so that only Arael could see it. Arael looked closely and saw a green-blue colored piece of crystal in Virgil's hand. Virgil smiled and quietly slipped it into Arael's hand without his permission.

"Mister Capello," Lady Agnes called.

"Yes ma'am!?" Virgil asked, turning his attention to the mentor.

"Your turn. Show them how it's done," Lady Agnes said, waving Virgil up eagerly.

Virgil winked at Arael before getting up and going to Lady Agnes. Arael opened his hand to look at the crystal, out of everyone else's sight. The crystal piece was beautiful, and it had a slight glow to it. Arael realized that this was a piece of the Aegis crystal that Virgil found! That crystal was valuable, and hard to chip! Did Virgil break his crystal, just to give this piece to him? He did know that Arael was struggling with Aegis.

Arael closed his hands around the crystal and then looked at Virgil again. Now he was really confused. Virgil was always nice to him, but his presence still felt odd to Arael. He'd gotten used to it, but he always felt it;

and now he found those forbidden spells that Virgil had been using. Nothing about him made any sense! Even the way that he reacted during Enzo's test was weird. Arael took another look at the crystal and then took a breath to make himself quit thinking about it so much. He could think about it after the Legion ceremony. Right now, he had to focus on himself.

"Ready?" Lady Agnes asked.

Arael watched as Virgil nodded to her in reply, and then Lady Agnes cast her spell. Virgil cast Aegis perfectly, destroying Lady Agnes's spell entirely. Aegis exploded into a huge, green wall of light, just like in the Grimwood Forest. Virgil's spell looked quite impressive, now that Arael had seen the other mages doing it.

"Showoff..." He heard one of the other mages mumble.

Arael looked over to the other mage and quietly giggled; he giggled partly at the mage's comment, and partly at Orias, who was sitting next to the same mage. Orias was leaning over his desk, half asleep, his dragon was dead to the world, and he was drooling on her head.

Lady Agnes clapped for Virgil, and then he returned to his seat. "See? Now that is how it's done!" She said. "That was the last of the mages, so... Mister Keon, let's start with you."

Arael stared at Lady Agnes for a moment. He wasn't expecting to be the first of the non-mages. He was nervous. He didn't want to fail... He was probably the worst in that entire class. Arael started sweating and his stomach felt sick, and then he felt Virgil tap on his shoulder again. Arael looked up at Virgil as he pointed to the crystal in his hand.

"You can do it," Virgil whispered.

Arael swallowed hard and then stood up and went to Lady Agnes. He gripped the crystal firmly in his hand, he couldn't decide if he wanted to risk using it or not. Arael stood in front of Lady Agnes and hid the crystal away.

"Ready?" Lady Agnes asked.

Arael nodded, "Yes ma'am."

Arael readied himself and then Lady Agnes cast her spell toward him. He tried his best and yelled out the spell, "Aegis!" He thought he might've gotten it, but it didn't work. Lady Agnes's spell knocked him flat on his butt.

"It's alright. Two more tries. Come on now." Lady Agnes ran across the room and quickly helped Arael up off of the floor.

Arael decided to try without the crystal again. He believed that he could do it… He tried to remember what Virgil did so that he could copy his movements. He honestly wasn't sure what he was doing wrong in the first place. He told Lady Agnes when he was ready and then she cast her spell at him again.

"Aegis!" Arael yelled…

There was a slight moment when he felt the spell working, but again, he got knocked down. Arael growled and then got up on his own. He looked at Virgil, as if he was asking if he should use the crystal. Virgil, mouthed the words 'use it, you can do it' to him in reply. Arael decided to take the crystal out and finally use it.

Arael nodded at Lady Agnes to signal that he was ready once again, and then she cast her spell for the last time. Arael watched the black magic approaching him. "Aegis!!!" He yelled, using the crystal. This time he felt a huge buzz of power explode from his body, as the light blasted forward and destroyed the dark magic. It wasn't as powerful as Virgil's Aegis, but it was definitely powerful enough. His Aegis was a dark gold color. He didn't quite expect to see it like that, but it was great! Arael smiled widely and then glanced between Virgil, Orias and Lady Agnes.

Lady Agnes clapped proudly. "Good, good, very good indeed!" She said.

Virgil clapped as well and smiled at Arael as he returned to his seat. Orias was still half asleep, so he didn't even see it... Arael sat down and then genuinely thanked Virgil, before trying to hand the crystal piece back.

Virgil refused it and insisted that Arael kept it. "It's a gift," he whispered.

Arael nodded and then looked at the crystal as he rolled it around in his hands. He was thankful for the help, but he felt a little bit guilty for cheating. The dark magic spells that Virgil had been casting came across his mind again, and then he thought about them deeply for a moment... He felt like he might've been over reacting. Maybe they weren't the exact same spells? Either way, Arael was stuck thinking for the rest of the day.

CHAPTER NINETEEN
That Dreaded Test

They were down to the second to last test now... But it was in the class that everyone was dreading the most... Combat class... Or Sir Adonis's class of horror, as Orias would call it... They were all going to be completely beat down by the end of all of this. Everyone hoped that they would have some downtime to recover. Hammurabi may have been able to fix their wounds, but not their mental states. There weren't many kids left in the castle that were still doing the tests to their highest skill. They all gave up.

The kids had their weapons with them and were headed to the combat room after breakfast. Arael and Orias didn't eat much, since they were stressed out and nervous. If Orias wasn't eating, then that really meant something... They passed Sir Enzo in the hallway as they walked.

"Good luck everyone," Enzo said, as he waved to them all.

Arael and Orias waved back and smiled halfheartedly... Enzo was patrolling the castle, as he'd been doing more and more often lately. He was still investigating what happened to Sir Cornelius. It was like the entire event that caused his death just vanished, and Enzo was afraid that whatever caused it was wandering the castle unnoticed. The kids weren't the only ones that were stressed and tired. The knights were too. They looked like they'd been getting even less sleep than the kids were.

"Do we really have to do this!?" Ego growled, as she walked up next to Orias. "Nobody's going to pass Adonis's class! The guy is unbeatable, it's absolutely ridiculous!"

Orias nodded. "I don't know if I can do this..." He said.

"Don't give up now, we're almost to the end, and then we'll surely get into the legions," Arael said, trying to lift Orias's spirits.

Orias held Nerida like a puppy, since she'd grown too big to sit on his shoulder over the past month. He looked at her and patted her head. "I don't know if I want to be a knight anymore..." Orias said.

"What!?" Arael exclaimed. "You can't give up just like that! You're a dragon rider for Zander's sake! If anybody is going to get into the legions it's going to be you! You. Have. A dragon! I'm just a boring helm..."

"But you have superpowers..." Orias said.

Suddenly, Ego grabbed Orias's ponytail and yanked it so he would look at her. "Listen, pinhead. I'm rooting for you, so you'd better not give up. If you get into the legions, I expect you to pick me as your protector," she said. "You got me?"

Orias wasn't sure if that was supposed to make him feel better or not. He pushed her away so she'd let go of his hair, and then looked to the floor. His cheeks got a little bit hot, since everybody was telling him that he was probably going to get picked for the legions. Ego was even rooting for him! ...Whatever that meant.

"Okay, I won't give up," Orias decided.

Ego roughly patted him on the back as they entered the combat room. Orias clenched his teeth at the rough pat, which felt more like a punch. Ego didn't know her own strength... Sir Adonis was standing on the dueling stage when they entered the combat room. He looked rather calm, as he always did. It was intimidating and comforting at the same time. Apparently some of the girls in the class thought that he was 'dreamy' and they giggled when they saw him. Arael thought it was disgusting. Sir Adonis could've been in his fifties for all they knew. And those girls were like, twelve... It didn't mean that they liked combat class though... Nobody did.

Sir Adonis stayed quiet and waited for the rest of the class to arrive. Arael had the Aegis crystal piece with him. He'd put it on a string the night before so that he could carry it around his neck; he had it hidden behind his shirt collar so nobody would see it. Arael looked around the room to see if he could spot Virgil, but he wasn't around for some reason.

"Have you seen Virgil?" Arael asked Orias.

Orias shook his head no in reply. That was weird... Virgil was always early. Arael decided to shrug it off, since he was late too sometimes. Maybe the Chancellor had to talk to Virgil.

Sir Adonis looked up at one of the windows near the high ceiling, and then turned toward the class. He stared at them for a moment, counting them with his eyes. His gaze shifted when Virgil finally walked in, and then he stopped counting the students. He always kept track of how many kids there were supposed to be, if there was one missing, he always knew it. Sir Adonis gripped the hilt of his sword and then cleared his throat loudly to get everyone's attention.

"Good day, students," he smiled slightly. "I can see it in your faces that you're not looking forward to this... Well, you shouldn't. I know that none of you like my way of teaching."

They stared at him silently, wondering why he was pointing out the obvious. They really just wanted to get this over with... Adonis walked to the edge of the dueling stage and crouched down so he could be closer to them. He spoke softly, "For today's test, you don't have to beat me at anything. All you have to do is perform good enough that I decide to pass you. Not that hard, right?" He smiled again.

The kids were once again confused. They stayed quiet and continued to stare at the intimidating man, as he stood up again and threw his arms out to his sides. "Impress me!" He said, in a louder, booming voice. Adonis took his sword out of its scabbard and spun it around a few times. "I asked permission from Sir Enzo, to use his magical arch. I'm sure you all know how that works by now... But he said no... So, I'll use my own magical relic. Let's see what it is, shall we?"

Adonis hopped off of the dueling stage and then went toward the back of the room. They all looked at each other apprehensively, and followed him to an area with some seats set up around an object that was covered by a large piece of cloth.

"This works about the same as Enzo's arch. I've had it around for years, but I brought it here just recently," Adonis explained, as he approached the covered object.

They watched as Sir Adonis grabbed the cloth and pulled it off of the object, revealing a grand, decorated mirror. Next, he demonstrated what it did, by touching it. His hand went through the glass, creating an odd effect. The glass looked like it was broken, and floating on top of gravity defying water. Once he pulled his hand out of it, the glass returned to normal. They had to admit that the mirror was pretty cool, but they were still nervous.

"Now... Don't bother grabbing your wooden weapons, because tests should only be done with the real thing," said Sir Adonis. "Don't be worried about injuries, they'll go away soon enough."

That didn't sound very convincing... Adonis looked the kids over again and then his gaze paused at Orias. He swung his sword around, and then pointed it at the boy.

Orias's eyes widened and he started shaking, with a cold sweat.

"You. You're the one that has been skipping my classes…" Adonis said. "Why don't you go first? You seem to believe that you know better than I."

Orias clutched his dragon tightly and refused to move… Arael looked at him and touched his shoulder to try and comfort him, while Sir Adonis waited patiently.

"It'll be okay, Orias. You can do it," Arael said.

Orias was still frozen, and then Ego and Virgil came to him at the same time. Virgil bent down and grabbed Orias's shoulders, while Ego stood behind him.

"Listen to me, Orias. You can do this. There's nothing that will stop you from passing this. Okay?" Virgil said, almost like a mother would.

"Yeah! Adonis is just a bully! You're better than him! You have a dragon and he doesn't!" Ego said loudly.

Adonis obviously heard what Ego said, but he didn't have a reaction to it. Ego meant for him to hear it anyway. Orias still wasn't listening, he just stayed frozen there. Virgil frowned and then Arael could almost see an idea pop into his head as he smiled again.

"Hey. Remember these three words, okay, buddy? Here they are: vis, virtus, animus," Virgil moved his finger in front of Orias's eyes with each of those three words. "They're words of courage, they always help me."

Orias blinked and then looked at Virgil, Ego and Arael, and then he nodded. "Okay… I can do it," he said, putting Nerida on the floor to wait with Virgil.

Orias finally stepped forward and went to Sir Adonis, who patted his shoulder.

"Good man," Adonis said, before gesturing toward the mirror for Orias to go in first.

Everyone watched as Orias walked through the mirror, followed by Adonis, and then they were gone. Once the mirror went back to normal, it didn't show anybody's reflections anymore. It must've been something it did when people were inside of it. Arael was nervous for Orias. He hoped that Adonis didn't hurt him too badly.

Arael watched as Virgil and Ego sat down, and then he sat with them before looking at Virgil skeptically. "You cast a spell on him, didn't you...?" He asked.

Virgil whipped his head around in surprise, and then shrugged. "Not really," he said.

"What does that even mean? You can't cast a 'not really' spell on somebody... You either cast a spell, or you didn't," Arael said.

"Okay, no. It was more of a psychological thing. Somebody I knew taught it to me a while back. It works quite well."

"You cast a spell..." Arael frowned.

"Yeah, I cast a spell," Virgil said.

"You're a dingleberry," Ego added.

Arael and Virgil laughed. Virgil nodded like he was agreeing with her. At least he knew that he was a dingleberry...

All of the students waited patiently for Orias to finish his test. Their hands were sweating and shaking with anxiety. Ego, Arael and Virgil hadn't spoken to each other much, since Orias went in. They were all busy thinking about how the test was going to go for them. Arael had his journal open in his lap and his charcoal pencil in his hand, but he was too nervous to even sketch.

"Half of the students have failed everything already," Ego said. "What happens if we aren't ready?"

That was the first time that they'd heard Ego express concern for this. Arael was surprised. Arael took a minute to think about it; he wasn't so sure how to answer, but he replied anyway, "I don't know. I think that Sir Adonis is too harsh on everyone. I mean, we haven't been here for too terribly long, so there's not much of a chance that we're ready for anything."

Ego frowned and looked at her balled up hands in her lap. "I just don't want to let the world down, you know? It may not seem like it, but this legion stuff is important to me. If the kids in this castle are meant to put an end to the Pneumati, then I want to be part of that and I want to destroy them with my own hands."

Virgil and Arael looked at her in thought. Arael could definitely relate. He felt almost exactly the same as she did. "Me too," Arael said, while Virgil nodded in agreement.

Just then, they saw the mirror change into that broken texture, as Orias emerged from it. Arael and Ego shot up from their seats eagerly.

"Well?" Ego asked.

Orias had a bloody lip and a black eye, but behind his injuries, he showed a smile and held up his weapon. "I passed! Barely..." He said.

"What!? You did!?" Arael was totally flabbergasted. He was happy for his friend, but again, he was flabbergasted. It gave him hope that everyone else might have a good chance to pass! "Congratulations! I knew you could do it!" Areal said as the other students clapped for Orias, while Nerida squeaked happily.

Orias smiled and sat down with the others as his injuries began to magically disappear. "Thanks for believing in me, guys," he said, looking at his friends.

Ego nodded as Virgil and Arael smiled at him in reply. Adonis walked out of the mirror next and then the students waited in suspense for the next person to be called. "Virgil, you're up," he announced.

Virgil's eyes lit up as he approached Adonis, he seemed to be the only student in the entire room that was even a little bit excited about the test. Everyone could tell that he wanted to unleash everything he had on Adonis, especially since he had his real weapons now.

"This should be too easy for you Virgil! You're good at everything!" Arael said.

That was probably the first positive thing that he'd said to Virgil. It felt good to be nice to him, after all that he'd done for not only Arael, but Orias too. Virgil turned around and smiled at Arael, before he walked into the mirror with Sir Adonis. They waited a while for Virgil to finish. He took a bit longer than Orias did, but eventually, Virgil came out with Adonis.

Arael, Orias and Ego looked up at him, waiting to know if he passed or not. Virgil cracked his neck with a pained smile on his face. He had a gash in his side and a cut on his hand that were both beginning to heal as he sat down.

"He said I passed with flying colors. I finally got him," Virgil laughed, almost maniacally.

Everyone looked at Sir Adonis, and saw a stab wound right below his sternum. Virgil had stabbed him with the end of his swallow wand, which would've been a killing blow in the real world. It was freaky that Adonis didn't care about the wound. He must've been able to ignore pain well. The wound healed up quickly either way, and then Adonis was ready to pick the next to be tested.

"Arael," Adonis said, pointing at him.

Ego, Orias and Virgil cheered for Arael as he stood up and went into the mirror. He had to take a deep breath to get himself into combat mode. He could do this. He could pass Adonis's test! Once Arael entered, he was met by a bright and empty room. It looked like the combat room, but it was all pure white with nothing inside. Arael looked around and then toward Adonis.

"Welcome, Arael," said Adonis.

"Thank you, Sir," Arael said, bowing to his mentor respectfully; he was trying to have more patience with Sir Adonis this time, for his own sake.

"These tests are hard for a reason. The fate of the future lies in your hands. Do you understand?" Said Adonis.

"Yes, Sir," Arael replied simply.

"Good." Adonis smirked oddly. "I know that you will become one of the greats... Now, there are no rules for you today, so unleash your full power on me. Use whatever magic you know. Use everything... Just know, that I'm not going to hold back either."

Arael nodded at Sir Adonis, sword in hand, waiting for his test to begin.

"Salute!" Adonis commanded. Arael stood straight across from Adonis and they saluted each other professionally. "Begin!"

Adonis attacked first, thrusting his sword toward Arael. Arael blocked the attack easily; he was trying his best to keep a straight face in order to show no weakness. Quickly, he counterattacked, knocking Adonis off balance.

"Good!" Adonis said, attacking again and again.

Arael's sword fighting skills had become quite good over time, and the little magic that he knew helped him greatly, enabling him to match the powerful Adonis. Adonis attacked Arael swiftly, aiming his sword straight for his chest, but Arael dodged it. Adonis continued to give Arael all that he had, unable to get a hit on him or play on his emotions. Or at least, Arael thought that he was giving him all that he had... Finally, Arael was able to knock Adonis's weapon away. Adonis frowned as he unexpectedly used magic to retrieve his sword. Adonis's frown changed to a smirk, as he flipped the sword around in his hand tauntingly. Arael was surprised that Sir Adonis was able to use that kind of magic at all!

Especially since he didn't even have to utter a word to make it work. What kind of magic was that?

Adonis attacked again, being easily blocked by Arael. He continued attacking from all directions, leaving Arael with no escape. Arael held his ground, blocking every attack and trying to counter with every opportunity that he could find, with not much luck. Adonis sliced a chunk of Arael's sleeve off, and then Arael whirled around and hit him with a weak Aegis spell, just to try and distract him. Adonis was able to attack Arael from behind, but he reacted quickly, reaching his arms over his head to protect his back with his sword. Adonis stayed where he was, pushing his sword against Arael's. Without warning, Adonis seemed to have disappeared, and before Arael could react a second time, he reappeared in front of him. Arael froze, still holding his sword behind him with shaking hands. Arael dropped his weapon and grabbed Sir Adonis's shoulders as he stood in front of him. Adonis's sword was plunged deep into his abdomen, dripping with blood.

"Wh-why?" Arael cried.

Sir Adonis slid his sword from Arael's flesh and stepped back, letting the boy fall to the ground.

"You passed, well done," Sir Adonis said emotionlessly, wiping the blood off of his sword with Arael's surcoat.

Arael desperately gasped for air, eyes wide and filled with tears as he gripped his wound.

"Oh please," Adonis clucked. "You'll have to go through much more pain than this if you are to become a knight. Come now, it's not real."

Adonis yanked Arael up off of the floor, and picked up his sword, dragging the boy's feet through his own blood. Arael choked from the pain as he cried and tried to escape from Adonis's grip. The man took him to the mirror and pushed him through. Virgil, Orias and Ego immediately stood up in excitement to see Arael, but were astonished when they saw that he was hurt so badly. Sir Adonis dropped Arael and his sword into the room, letting him hit the floor roughly.

"Ego," Adonis said, brushing Arael off completely.

"Arael!" Orias yelled.

Arael couldn't speak until his wound closed up. He gasped loudly in relief when it was gone. That had to have been the worst pain that he felt in his life. Ego ignored Adonis's call to wait until she knew that Arael was okay, while everyone else stared at him lying on the ground.

Arael gasped one more time before letting them know that he was going to be okay. "I'm alright... I passed," he wheezed.

Everyone clapped, and then Virgil helped him up off of the ground. Arael couldn't believe how much being stabbed with a sword hurt – a big sword at that. He would be glad when he could wear armor to protect himself. He didn't care how heavy the armor was, he just didn't want to get stabbed again.

Ego congratulated him, and then hesitantly went into the mirror, glancing back at him one more time. Arael was so glad Adonis's test was over, and he had passed. Now he only had one last test before he could be a knight! Even though he got hurt, he felt like it was a lesson all on its own. Now he knew what being stabbed was like, and he definitely learned from that experience. Arael looked at Virgil and Orias, and then toward the mirror after Ego disappeared. A certain realization hit him, and he believed that he'd figured out what he had to do to outlast Enzo's final test.

CHAPTER TWENTY
The Moment of Truth

Arael gathered Orias, Ego and Virgil, and told them what he thought they must do, in order to get through Enzo's test. He said that he believed they had to find each other and work together. Virgil agreed completely. It made sense because they made a full legion all together and that's how it should've been all along. Ego was the protector, Virgil was the mage, Orias was the rider and Arael was the helm. Everyone was willing to give Arael's plan a try. Virgil told them about a huge tree that could easily be seen from the river, so they were going to meet there…

Once Arael entered the arch, he looked around to get a sense of his surroundings. This time, he appeared near the buried tower. He vaguely remembered where the river was from there, so he headed off in that general direction. Arael was careful whenever he heard the voices of other students, and this time he checked the trees too, knowing that they could've been anywhere.

He kept on walking until he found the river, and then it took him over two hours, before he could find the tree that Virgil spoke of. Arael was happy when he saw that Ego was waiting there, so he hadn't wandered to the wrong place. This tree shouldn't have been easy to miss though, since it was the most enormous tree in the Grimwood Forest.

Ego greeted him and then they found a good place to sit, so that they could wait for the other two. It didn't take long for some unwanted guests to find them, but Ego quickly scared them off after striking down one of their buddies. Arael was always impressed by how terrifyingly strong Ego was. It wasn't just her strength that impressed him, but everything. She was truly unlike anyone else. All four of them were unique in their own ways.

After waiting for a while, they saw Virgil coming toward them, with Orias and Nerida by his side. Arael was excited when everybody was together. He almost felt like he was with family. That was the first time he'd felt so comfortable since he left his father. When they were all together, there was a feeling of invincibility that came over them. This time, whenever the arch threw an obstacle their way, there was no stopping them. They handled the obstacles like they were nothing but a small rock on the pathway. The time that they spent out in the forest was quite enjoyable, almost like camping.

The team stayed near the big tree, because it was excellent protection from the elements. With their combined knowledge, they knew just about everything. This must've been what being in a legion was like; together they were like one. The team waited out the hours, until they came to the last two, which were the problem hours for Arael and Virgil the last time. They found out that it was Ego's downfall the last time too. She had taken a spill off of a cliff when the Pneumati came along and surrounded her.

It was dark now, and the only light that they had was from Virgil's Illustro spell. They were sitting back to back under the tree, ready for the Pneumati to show up. They were nervous, but they felt a lot better now that they had each other.

"There's no way anyone is going to bring us down this time," Ego said quietly.

Orias nodded and laughed as he drew a picture of his dragon in the dirty snow while she posed in front of him. "Yeah! Why didn't we do this before?"

"Oh, I don't know... I probably would've tried to kill you guys the last time," Ego said.

Everyone chuckled, and then they heard a twig snap nearby. They immediately looked up, with their weapons in hand. They didn't see anything, but that didn't mean that there was nothing there.

Arael looked at the sky, where a sliver of the moon was visible through the tree branches. "It's about that time..." He said.

"Alright guys, remember that Aegis is your best bet on this, but use it sparingly, because it drains your energy," Virgil said.

Orias was able to cast Aegis to an extent, which was enough to do some damage to the Pneumati. They were going to have to rely mostly on Virgil and Ego for that though. Because Ego was a protector, her Aegis spell was automatically strong like Virgil's. Arael's wasn't quite as good as he thought it was, even with the crystal piece that he had, but it would have to do.

Virgil stood up and looked around, so everyone else did so as well. They all waited quietly for something to happen, and then Arael got a vision. The vision showed them and the Pneumati, but he knew what it meant.

"They're here," Arael said.

Everyone readied their weapons and then sure enough, a Pneumati came barreling out of the darkness from Ego's side. "Aegis!" Ego yelled, putting the creature to an immediate stop with her maroon colored spell.

Everyone nodded and continued to stand their ground. They were going to wait for the Pneumati to come to them; there was no use in running around blindly through the forest. The trees around them seemed to have come alive as the Pneumati started to stir. It was slow at first; they were only met by one Pneumati every few minutes, but the numbers were increasing. Virgil hit them with the Aegis crystal, knocking their heads off of their shoulders. Ego demolished them with her sword. Orias hit them with his axe, while Nerida alerted him whenever she felt it was the right moment to strike, and Arael sliced them to pieces with his sword. They didn't have the need to use Aegis for quite a long time, until they became completely surrounded. The team had a plan though.

When the Pneumati closed in on them, Arael waited until the right moment to give the word. "Do it now!" He said.

"Aegis!" In unison, they cast the spell.

It was enough to destroy almost every single enemy that surrounded them. Their plan had worked perfectly. Finally, when they thought they saw an end to the Pneumati, they broke away from each other to take care of the remaining stragglers. Each of them paused to scan their surroundings when they couldn't see any more Pneumati, and when they were sure that there were no more left, they regrouped.

"That was incredible! I can't believe we did that! We're like gods!" Orias said, jumping around in excitement.

"I knew that there had to be a secret to this thing! We made that look so easy!" Arael said.

"Yes!" Ego exclaimed, as she and Virgil pulled everyone into a quick group hug.

"Gosh, I'm just so happy right now!" Orias said, wiping a tear from his eye. "How much longer do we have, Arael?"

Arael looked at the sky, but before he could answer, they had suddenly appeared in the field, outside of the magic arch. The four stared wide eyed when they saw the entire class of Mountainglaive standing in front of them, with colorful Illustro lights floating about! They were all cheering for them! Lady Agnes was there, Sir Gwenael, even Sir Adonis was there!

"We did it!?" Ego said in astonishment.

"We made it!" Orias said.

Arael looked to the side, and saw that only five others had successfully made it through the test with them. They were standing in a line with Arael's group.

The Chancellor was standing with the crowd before them, clapping with a big smile on her face. "Congratulations on passing the final test!" She said. "I thought that this called for a little celebration!"

Sir Enzo came out of the crowd and personally congratulated them all with hugs. "Let's give them a ride to their quarters, shall we!?" He yelled out.

Everyone came to the students who passed the test and picked them up as they continued to cheer. It was such a great feeling! Arael, Orias, Virgil and even Ego had never felt so important or proud! Virgil grabbed Arael's hand and shook it in respect, and then they all thrusted their fists into the air to celebrate with everyone else, until they were carried all the way to their rooms. What a day it was!

CHAPTER TWENTY ONE
The Legions

"Trust me, trust me, trust me, trust me," the voice whispered over and over. It wouldn't stop. There was blood, Pneumati, horrible things. "Don't let them!" The voice screamed. Suddenly, there was a pale boy, with black hair. He did nothing but stare. He was locked up in a cage. "Promise you'll end it?" The boy asked, with a different voice than the last one. The boy's head twitched violently and then his face appeared to be horribly wounded. His eyes bled, his mouth bled, his nose bled... There were drops of blood falling into a pool of milky white liquid that had a horrible energy to it, while the screams of a thousand children bubbled up from the deep, dark bottom...

Arael quickly sat up in his bed and glanced around. He'd been dreaming again... He wiped sweat off of his brow with the back of his hand and then took a breath. These dreams were not enjoyable... He wondered who that boy with the black hair was. He'd never seen him before; he hadn't seen anything that appeared in that dream before. It had to be one of those Dreamwalker things again. Arael still couldn't figure out who the 'trust me' voice belonged to, it was becoming quite a bother to him.

Arael stared at the dark red blanket over his legs. His journal next to him had new sketches of the boy with black hair, and the scenes from his dream. This day was the day... The day that the legions were going to be decided. He was much less excited about it than he thought he would be. He was scared more than anything. His gut felt tight with the bubbling juices of anxiety... Arael's eyes shifted when he heard Orias roll over in the bed nearby. He watched as Orias slowly opened his eyes and then suddenly shot up from the bed in excitement, waking up everyone else in the room, including his dragon, who was sleeping under the bed.

"Today's the day, today's the day!!!" Orias sang. He ran to Arael and pulled on his hand. "Come on, Arael! Get your boots on! Get your sword and surcoat! We're going to be knights!"

"Don't be so sure... It's a one in a thousand chance," said one of the boys in the room, as he rubbed his eyes drowsily.

Orias ignored him and then ran off to get dressed, leaving Nerida under his bed. The dragon poked her head out, looking around in confusion, before making a grumpy little dragon noise and curling up back under the bed. Arael laughed and shook his head before going to get dressed.

Once everyone was done getting ready for the day, they went down to the dining hall, as they did every morning. There was already food waiting for them on the table, and Virgil and Ego were already seated. Ego spotted Arael and Orias and waved them down. "Hey, guys!" She called. Arael and Orias sat down with Virgil and Ego, in front of plates with fresh bread, ham, and pink fruit juice to go with it. Orias tore right into the food as soon as his butt hit the bench.

"I can't believe the legion ceremony is finally happening!" Ego said.

"I know! I'm so excited!" Orias said, spitting food everywhere.

"I wish you all the best of luck," Virgil smiled.

Arael stayed quiet. He was in his own mind... He felt so distant this day, like there was something about to happen that he really wasn't looking forward to. It may have just been the lingering feeling that hung on to him from the dream... Another explanation could've been that he was just tired. He seemed to have lost time, missing all of breakfast. The only thing that snapped him out of it was Chancellor Hofmeister's voice.

"Attention students!" The Chancellor said happily. "Today we will be traveling to Tarragon for the Legion ceremony, for that is where we will meet our very own legion masters! I'm sure you'll be very excited to venture somewhere outside of the castle for the first time in ages!"

They all cheered; of course they were excited! Even Arael perked up and smiled. They were going to get to experience something different now, and they were about to meet the legion masters!!!

"I'm sure you've had enough time to eat your breakfast, so we'll be heading off. We need to leave here early in order to make it to Tarragon on time. I expect you all to stay with the elder knights as we travel," said the Chancellor. "I'd like to let you know, that no matter who is chosen, you all will still be equally as important here at Mountainglaive, and we will never think any less of you, my beautiful children... Now, let us head off, shall we?"

They immediately stood up and started to follow the elder knights to the front of the castle, where they had arrived on the first day. The younger kids were loaded into the carriages, while the older kids were expected to walk on their own. Orias was young enough to have been able to ride in one of the carriages. Once everyone was ready, they all headed off. Arael looked back as they went down the path, high above the salty blue water, and watched as the castle began to look like a mountain once again. It was truly mesmerizing.

It took longer than they expected to get inside of Tarragon's perimeter. Once they did though, the kids gasped in awe. The kingdom looked different from afar because it was surrounded by a magic barrier to help keep it protected from the Pneumati. There was a grand castle in the center of the kingdom that had flags with the twelve symbols of the legion masters on them, and as they made their way through the kingdom, people let them through politely and waved. It was odd to see adults other than the elder knights and the chancellor after all that time. Arael almost expected to see his dad among the crowd... Tarragon was beautiful, and it was clearly a rich place. Many of the students had never seen anything quite like it before, since they were used to the poor villages that had been picked clean by the Pneumati.

"This is amazing!" Ego gasped from behind Arael.

Arael smiled back at her and then looked up at the castle as they stopped in front of it. Everyone waited for the younger kids to get out of the carriages, and then Sir Enzo strode to the huge, open doors of the castle.

"Welcome to the castle of the twelve masters!" Enzo said excitedly.

Enzo proudly walked through the doors, arm in arm with the Chancellor, as everyone else followed them inside. This castle was even more amazing than Mountainglaive – though it was much smaller in size. There were gold things everywhere! Real life gold! The elder knights stopped the kids in front of a stage, where twelve thrones were displayed, along with twelve people sitting in them. Each of the twelve people wore a symbol and color of each legion. It was them! The legion masters!

Arael's mouth hung open in a whole mixture of emotions. He was definitely excited now! This is what he'd been working up to this entire time! Since most of the students had given up on the tests and failed them, he had a great chance to be chosen for a legion! Arael looked up at the man who wore the same colors and symbol as he did. That was Legion Master Ariese! Ariese looked very old and stern faced, he was quite skinny, and he had no hair. He looked a lot different than Arael expected; he imagined that he was going to be more like Sir Enzo.

After a moment, all of the legion masters stood up and walked to the front of the stage. Leodegrance was the first to speak, "Good day, young helms, riders, mages, protectors, healers and beyond of Mountainglaive," she started. "Today is a very important day for all of us. Today is the day that we choose some of the new guardians of the land. Each of the twelve legion masters has monitored your overall progress in Mountainglaive. One knight has been carefully chosen to represent each legion. Those knights will then choose three comrades to fill the remaining positions left in their represented legion. We are honored to be in your presence."

Next, some people that were lined up against the walls began playing loud instruments, making grand music echo throughout the room. Arael looked around and saw that Tarragon's people had gathered in the castle to watch. This was a much bigger deal than they had ever imagined, it was almost terrifying. Arael glanced up at the legion masters as the first in line picked up his weapon and then the music became softer. The first in line was Geminiano. Geminiano was a rough looking man, whose face was covered in scars; his legion color was yellow, and his symbol was two human figures standing side by side. Virgil, Ego and Orias came through the crowd to join Arael, and then Ego put her arm over Orias's shoulders, while she held Virgil's hand. Arael looked at them while they all smiled, and Orias put his hand on his shoulder. They were all nervous, but they were also hopeful for each other. Arael didn't feel so alone in this with them around. They felt butterflies and angry bees in their stomachs as they waited for their legion masters to step forward.

"I'm so excited, I feel like I'm going to poop my pants!" Orias exclaimed, unable to stand still.

Eleven of the legion masters stepped back and let Geminiano call out who he had chosen for his legion. Geminiano looked around for a moment, holding onto his wooden mage's staff. The kids held their breath, ready to hear who the first to be chosen would be.

"The knight chosen to represent the legion of Geminiano will be the rider, Fikri Schlimm," he proclaimed.

Arael, Orias, Ego and Virgil were all shocked. They weren't expecting that at all. They watched as Schlimm jumped up onto the stage and thrusted his fists into the air, causing the crowd to cheer wildly for him. If Schlimm got into the first legion then Arael's group must've had huge chances to be picked. Arael was almost angry that Schlimm was picked for a legion, and then he continued to pick three other dunderheads that Geminiano then dubbed official knights. As soon as Geminiano tapped each of their shoulders with his weapon, their uniforms changed to his color and symbol. Geminiano must've had the same idiotic mindset as his new legion... People always chose like minds.

Next up was Scorpios, Ego's legion master. Ego's legion master looked just as tough as she was. Virgil squeezed Ego's hand as Scorpios stepped forward, with her huge sword in hand. Ego's hands were shaking as she held her breath, hoping for her name to be called up.

"The knight chosen to represent the legion of Scorpios is the protector," Scorpios started, causing the four to lean forward with even more hope for Ego, "Waldo Werner," she finished.

Ego finally breathed and then looked down at the floor in disappointment before stomping her foot. "Meadow muffins!" She yelled.

Orias and Virgil patted her shoulders to try and comfort her while the next two legion masters were picking their knights. It felt like it took forever. The suspense was killing them all. It would've been a lot faster if they didn't have to be so disgustingly proper about it. The next legion master to step forward was Orias's – Sagia. Sagia was a dumpy little woman, who was funny to look at.

"I have chosen the helm, Yvonne Wulf, to represent the legion of Sagia," she decided.

"D'aw..." Orias said in disappointment. "But I thought I did good..."

Ego gave Orias a hug, as the next few legion masters picked their knights. They were all happy to have each other for comfort. It didn't feel like a complete loss now that they were all friends. Arael stared at Ariese, trying to somehow force him with his mind to consider choosing him. He thought for sure that Orias and Ego had a chance. There was no way that Arael was going to get turned down though, he knew it! Virgil, Orias and Ego grabbed onto Arael's arms and shoulders as Ariese came forward to choose his knight.

"You're for sure going to get picked, Arael. I know it," Virgil smiled.

"Yeah! You're the best here!" Orias said, shaking Arael's arm.

Arael nodded. If Virgil said that he was going to get into the legion, then it must have been true. Everything else that Virgil said had been true so far. Arael didn't receive any visions about it either, so he just had to be destined to be chosen! He was so serious about being a knight! He wanted it more than anyone else! Arael stared at Ariese and then unexpectedly made eye contact with him as he gripped the hilt of his sword so tight that it hurt. The two locked gazes, until Ariese began to speak. "The knight that will represent the legion of Ariese, will be Arial Erkens, the mage," Ariese decided.

Arael had to backtrack for a moment to process what had just happened. He thought for sure that Ariese had just said his name, but it wasn't his name! It was a girl named Arial! What!? How could that be!? He wasn't even aware of this girl's existence! Arael froze, unable to believe that he wasn't the one up on that stage.

"What!?" Orias exclaimed, throwing his hands up in the air. "What!?"

"This garbage is screwed up. None of this is right," Ego growled.

Virgil stepped in front of Arael and put his hand on his shoulder, sharing the feeling of disappointment with him. They all knew how hard Arael had worked for this, and it seemed like all of their hard work meant nothing to these so called legion masters. Arael's eyes felt like they were going to explode with tears, but he held them in. He felt stupid for being so upset about it, especially since Schlimm got picked and not him. Even stupid Giro and Grob were in Schlimm's legion! None of this was fair! Not one bit!

Arael pushed Virgil's hand off of his shoulder and started walking away, so he could sit down at the back of the crowd. He was done with this whole thing. Most of all, he felt he was being robbed of the chance to be the person he wanted to be for his father.

"Arael, come back!" Ego said.

"Arael?" Orias said, grabbing Arael's hand. "Arael, stop."

Arael turned and looked at Orias silently. He didn't know why either of them were trying to stop him. They all had just experienced the biggest disappointment ever!

"Look, Arael, look!" Ego called.

Arael looked at Ego and then up at the legion masters. He didn't even want to think about them anymore. Leodegrance was announcing her pick now; he didn't even hear who it was, but it was too late anyway. Arael frowned and tried to walk away again, but his friends continued to yell at him.

"Arael! Hurry up and go up there!" Ego said.

Arael was about to ask her what on Domhan she was talking about, but then he paused and noticed that everybody was looking at him. He didn't know why until he looked up at the stage, finally noticing that Leodegrance was standing with Virgil next to her. Arael had forgotten all about Virgil. Of course he got chosen. Why wouldn't he have been? He was perfect for the legions. Arael stared wide eyed, and then Leodegrance must've repeated what Arael had missed, "Arael Keon, you've been chosen by Sir Virgil Capello as the helm of my legion."

Arael looked between Ego and Orias and slowly made his way up to the stage. He felt even more like an idiot now, but he did it completely to himself this time. Arael passed Schlimm, and the rest of the legions standing on the stage before stopping next to Virgil. Arael looked up at Virgil as the boy smiled down warmly at him, and then chose the rest of his legion members. Arael was in so much shock that he didn't hear who Virgil was choosing, but he had an idea of who they were. He just stared at the boy before him, as Ego and Orias joined them. Arael couldn't believe that Virgil picked him to be in his legion. He didn't owe him anything at all…

All of them kneeled to Leodegrance as she dubbed them official knights. The tingling feeling that Arael had felt when he got his Ariese decorations crept through his body, as the red ram of Ariese was replaced with the golden lion of Leodegrance. Arael could feel the roar of the crowd as they clapped for them, cheering for their new guardians. Even though Ego, Orias and Arael didn't get picked by the legion masters, they still got to be knights. The best thing was that they got to be knights all together. Maybe it was a good thing that they didn't get picked by the other legion masters. They seemed like jerks anyway…

Arael felt Ego grab his hand and looked at everyone else. They were all holding hands together. They were the most united out of all the legions. Once the last few knights were chosen, the legion of Leodegrance all raised their joined fists into the air to celebrate righteously with the crowd while the music boomed loudly. What a grand celebration!

Through the loud merriment, Arael thought that he heard a girl's scream. He looked around, unsure of if it was a real scream or not. It was hard to know what was going on through the chaos of the celebration. Arael looked over at his new legion and by the looks of their faces, they'd heard something unusual too.

"What was that? Do you see anything?" Arael asked loudly.

Ego shrugged as she scanned the area. Virgil didn't look as engaged in the celebration as he was before at all. In fact, he was staring at the ground with wide, teary eyes as if he had suddenly become horrified.

"Virgil, what's wrong!?" Arael tried to get his voice through the uproar.

All of a sudden, the entire legion of Pisceros was attacked by something. The music stopped and everyone screamed as Pisceros was quickly killed off, along with their legion master. Next, Scorpios was attacked, then Librona and Aquarius! It all went so fast that nobody was able to react.

"Everybody to safety!" Enzo yelled. "Fight back, legions!"

The legion of Leodegrance drew their weapons for the first time as a team when Pneumati began flooding into the castle. The Pneumati grabbed some of the students of Mountainglaive and took them away, killing any adults who tried to stop them. Some of the legion masters fought back, while others backed out and cast Defugio to escape. What kind of legion masters were they if they were fleeing!? Arael couldn't believe his eyes! Those cowards!

A few kids nearby were being attacked by the evil creatures, so Arael and his legion jumped off the stage and slayed them, turning them to into the black tar that they were. Ego grabbed the kids and pushed them toward Lady Agnes and the Chancellor, who were casting Defugio on small groups of the kids to get them out of there! The other legions weren't helping much. Most of them were too scared! Virgil and Ego worked together and cast Aegis on the Pneumati, getting rid of a large group of the creatures so that more of the kids could have a path to escape. One of the Pneumati screeched like a banshee, toward Virgil, along with some odd whispering noises. Virgil hit it in the face with his swallow wand, and then stabbed it, not before yelling, "Shut up!"

Sir Adonis came barreling through the crowd, taking down every Pneumati in his path. None of them were able to even get close to him. He helped some more kids get away as he continued to destroy the Pneumati. The legion of Leodegrance got split up, but they were fighting the Pneumati to the best of their abilities. Virgil had to escape some of the creatures to go help Orias before they could take him away. Aegis spells were flying everywhere! Arael turned just as he saw some Pneumati sneaking up behind Virgil while he was distracted.

"Virgil, look out!" Arael said. Arael grabbed the Aegis crystal piece from around his neck so he could get rid of the Pneumati behind Virgil.

"Wait, Arael, don't!" Virgil panicked.

It was too late though, Arael had already cast Aegis. Virgil ran and tried to get out of the way of the spell that was blasted his way. The spell instantly killed three of the Pneumati and hit Virgil's leg. Aegis couldn't hurt people though, only dark beings. Arael paused in confusion when Virgil suddenly barked in pain and began limping. He tried to recover and struck down a few more of the Pneumati, ignoring what had just happened. Adonis saw this too, so Arael knew that he wasn't going crazy.

"You little cretin!" Adonis snarled. "I knew it!"

Adonis suddenly went after Virgil and swung his sword at him. Virgil cast an Aegis spell toward the Pneumati and then turned around and blocked Adonis, but it caught him off guard and knocked him down.

"Get off!" Virgil yelled as he blocked another swing from Adonis, getting the sword stuck in the wood of his swallow wand.

Arael stood nearby, uncertain of what to do. He saw Ego ram through a crowd of Pneumati and then punch Adonis off of Virgil. "What are you doing!? Attack the Pneumati, not him, you rotten mouth fart!" She yelled.

Arael remembered all of the bad vibes and visions of the Pneumati he had that seemed to always involve Virgil, and now he finally knew why he had them. "He is Pneumati," Arael said. "Aren't you!?" He yelled, looking at Virgil.

Virgil looked betrayed, but he didn't answer Arael's question. Instead, he continued to fight the creatures with everyone else. Arael decided to fight too, but he wasn't done with Virgil yet. Enzo and Sir Gwenael came to Arael's legion, and then put up their shields. "Fruke is casting Aegis Armis! Get down!" Enzo shouted.

Arael looked to Virgil. If he really was Pneumati, then that spell was going to kill him. Arael was worried, but he was angry too. Virgil looked at Arael in panic and then grabbed his shirt and shook him.

"You have to trust me, Arael! I'm not like them!" He shouted. Suddenly, two Pneumati came out of Defugio right behind Virgil and grabbed him. "Please, Arael!" Virgil yelled again, trying to pull away from the Pneumati.

"Wait!" Arael said with wide eyes. "Wait!"

He swung his sword at the Pneumati, but they disappeared with Virgil as soon as the sharp metal met the Pneumati's cloak. Quickly, Arael heard the Chancellor yell out the Aegis Armis spell, and then an enormous, powerful red pulse exploded throughout the entire castle, and beyond. All of the Pneumati instantly screeched and dissolved into nothing but dust in the wind, leaving only the beings of light behind. Everything was silent now... The creatures were gone... Some of the students were gone... And Virgil was gone too...

Arael stared straight ahead, and finally recognized the 'trust me' voice from his dreams and visions... He didn't understand why he didn't know before; why he couldn't have seen this coming even when it was handed right to him.

"It was a trap all along," Sir Adonis said, before pointing his dirty finger at Enzo. "You let that little Pneumati shite into this!"

"Me?" Enzo asked in astonishment. "What on Domhan are you talking about!?"

"Virgil Capello was one of them this whole time! He was probably the one who murdered your last Combat trainer!" Adonis yelled.

Orias ran to Adonis and pushed him as Nerida nipped at his knees. "He didn't kill him! I was there!" He said.

"How do you know, boy!? Pneumati have no limit to the magic that they can do!" Adonis argued.

"He's gone now. So you don't have to worry about it anymore," Arael said starkly.

"Arael!?" Ego said in astonishment.

"No! We have to worry even more now, because he could disclose the location of Mountainglaive!" Adonis roared. "Don't you understand!?"

"Enough!" The Chancellor said as she pushed through the crowd. "Arguing is not going to fix anything. We just lost half of our students to the Pneumati! We need to get the rest of them back to the castle before anything else happens... I knew that this was a mistake..." She glared at Ariese, who had done nothing but watch the chaos unfold the entire time.

Everyone nodded in agreement, and then went to work. Orias and Ego couldn't believe what was going on. They looked at Arael in disapproval before running to catch up with Enzo so they could try to talk to him about this. Arael couldn't believe it either...

CHAPTER TWENTY TWO
Dark Secrets

The Pneumati came out of Defugio, appearing in a terrible, swampy place. This hell was called Blightmire. It was a place that was far away from any real civilization, and it was a forbidden land that the Pneumati had called home for almost as long as they had existed. The Pneumati had all of the kids that they'd just stolen with them, including Virgil.

One of the younger kids, who was crying with a runny nose looked up at Virgil. "What are they going to do to us, Virgil? I don't want to die!" The kid asked.

"You're not going to die, okay? Everything is going to be alright," Virgil told him. The other kids began taking notice that he was there as well, and started screaming and yelling at him to help. Virgil didn't know what to do to help them. He hadn't been able to do anything before, and he knew that. "You're getting out of here, I promise, just hang on," Virgil said softly.

It was a promise that he was never able to keep, but the comfort of hope was always better than nothing. The Pneumati pushed Virgil in a different direction than the other kids, and they screamed for him to come back. It made Virgil's heart hurt.

The cold, muddy ground squished under their feet as they walked. The décor of the place was mostly composed of bones, and it smelled of death... The sky there was always dark, and the surrounding trees were all sharp and rotten. There were pools of white liquid called Marrow Pits, which were concoctions of many things, evil things that were put together by the Pneumati, and all of the things that they had stolen. The Marrow Pits burned anyone that wasn't Pneumati like the hottest fire. The Pneumati bathed and even slept in it, like it was the sweat of gods; it didn't burn them anymore, once they were pure darkness.

One of the Pneumati next to Virgil spoke to him in whispering noises. Virgil could understand, but he refused to speak the language of the Pneumati. The language itself came with its own dark attributes. One of the Pneumati grabbed onto the hood of its cloak and pulled it away from its head. The Pneumati had revealed its face to Virgil, but he'd seen it before. He was all too familiar with the faces of these two Pneumati. This one was female, and her face was as pale as a corpse. Her lips had a purple tone to them, and her hair was as light as Virgil's. Her eyes even glowed a bright violet color.

"You're finally home, brother," she said, with a shrill, strained voice, unlike any human. "Why did you choose to fight us?"

"You know exactly why. Don't play that game with me, Zillah..." Virgil said. He was scared, but something about this felt different than the last time he'd been in Blightmire. He was angry now. He was tired of the Pneumati's games.

"Don't disrespect her!" Said the other Pneumati, as he took his hood off as well, revealing what looked like a ghostly white skull, covering the dark black magic hiding underneath. Black ribbons of magic floated from his head like smoke, and his eyes glowed fiery orange.

"Shut up!" Virgil yelled. "Aegis!" He cast the spell at him, burning his Pneumati flesh.

"Malachi!" Zillah yelled, before burning Virgil with her own power in return.

Virgil fell to his knees, trying to bear the pain of the magic while Malachi healed himself with his own magic, for he was born a healer. Zillah would've been fit to be a rider, but they were both corrupt. Malachi was not vulnerable to Aegis because of his powers.

"Father isn't going to be pleased with you. Always acting up like this!" Malachi growled.

"How could you have run away from home?" Zillah asked. "Always the problem child... I don't understand why you're still father's favorite."

"What makes you think I'm his favorite!? He hates me! He tortures me every day! Is that what you want!?" Virgil yelled in Zillah's face.

Malachi punched Virgil forward to make him walk. They took him to a poorly made 'castle' that was nothing more than rotten logs, branches and stones that were stacked up on top of each other. There were holes and openings in it, but it never collapsed. It was twenty stories high, and some old, twisted trees had grown into it, which served as its support. Virgil's pureness was so out of place here. Nobody would ever have guessed that this had been his home for his entire life. They walked straight into the hazardous structure, where there was a huge Marrow Pit in the middle of the makeshift vestibule. The floor was dirt, and there was a slope that led straight into the pit.

"Father! Virgil has returned!" Zillah yelled with a psychotic tone to her words.

They watched the white liquid, as a lump grew in the center. The liquid had the consistency of thick, wet sand. The lump grew until whatever was under it was standing up tall enough for it to start dripping off, revealing a humanly figure. The figure stood up straight, still completely covered in white. The pool was waist deep, but the figure was easily seven feet tall. The figure suddenly dipped down and then turned into the blackest of smoke, leaving all of the white liquid behind. The black smoke reformed as a dark, ghostly man in front of Virgil. It put its face right up near his and looked into his soul with its turquoise eyes. Its face was recognizable as human, but it was a lot like Malachi's face, and eyes couldn't focus on the constant movement of its unstable structure. The creature had destroyed and put itself back together so many times in order to become this ... thing ... that it had become something unworldly, a heinous abomination.

"My son," it said, with a low, growly voice that could send chills down anyone's spine.

"Ocharos..." Virgil frowned.

"Why so angry?" The creature smiled menacingly, with sharp, grey teeth. It was the king of the Pneumati himself, Dieudonne, Ocharos... "You've never addressed me that way before... Have you been hanging out with the wrong crowd?" He laughed. Virgil only stared at Ocharos angrily, with no reply. "How did your mission go? Did you find the location of the crimson spirit's refugee camp?" Ocharos asked, referring to the Chancellor and Mountainglaive, as he put his hands behind his back and started slowly circling his offspring.

"Mission? You mean, you made him leave!?" Zillah asked.

"No. But I knew where he was going at all times. So now, one of us knows where it is. The prisoners never last long enough to give us what we want. He knew very well that he can't escape me," Ocharos answered.

"Ah! You're a genius, father!" Zillah laughed.

"So? Where is it, Virgil?" Malachi asked.

Virgil glared at the ground. "I don't know what you're talking about," he said.

Ocharos suddenly lashed out at him and grabbed his throat, picking him up off of the ground. "Do not play dumb with me, boy! You bear the symbol of Leodegrance, do you not!?" Ocharos growled, pulling at the golden decorations on Virgil's surcoat. "You are a terrible liar and you always have been! So, tell me now… Where. Is. Mountainglaive…?"

Virgil refused to say anything, but it was obvious that he was terrified. Ocharos held him up for a moment as he stared at him, silently judging his son's inferiority. He wanted to give him a chance to reveal the answer that he was looking for, but Virgil still wouldn't say a thing. Ocharos scowled and then tossed Virgil against the wall. Surprisingly, the logs and stones held up, instead of falling on top of him.

Ocharos shook his head in disappointment. "Why must it always be a fight?" He asked. "Wouldn't it just be easier to give in? My eldest, I have been waiting for you to join my side for so many years, yet you continue to keep me waiting. I have been very patient with you."

Virgil got up off of the ground and approached Ocharos in annoyance, before telling him exactly what was on his mind, "We go through this every time. You know my answer! So, what'll it be today, huh? Burns? Bruises? Are you going to snap my legs? Come on! Give me all you have, 'father!' It's just going to end the same as always!"

This was the first time that Virgil had expressed so much rage and defiance. Especially toward Ocharos; in fact, it caught Ocharos by surprise. Running away from this hell hole was the best decision that Virgil had ever made… He only hoped that he could hold in the precious information that Ocharos wanted, so he could protect everyone at Mountainglaive… He never realized how much he really hated Ocharos until now. Ocharos paused for a moment to think, and then he scoffed at Virgil's outburst before pounding him in the head with his fist, knocking him to the floor.

"Get him out of my sight..." Ocharos commanded. "Force him to tell you where the castle is."

Malachi and Zillah nodded and then yanked Virgil up off of the ground to take him up to one of the rooms in their castle. It was going to be a long painful night...

CHAPTER TWENTY THREE

What to Do, What to Do...?

It was afternoon back at Mountainglaive, seven days later... The elder knights and the Chancellor had been speaking with the remaining legion masters to try and figure out what they were to do. Everything had been put on hold... The Chancellor had her own set of plans and beliefs, but unfortunately, even though she ran Mountainglaive, she was still under the rule of the legion masters. The masters were not the people that everyone once respected. They felt so alone now that they knew they were being controlled by these selfish cowards who called themselves great people.

The sun shone dark, fiery orange through all of the windows. The light was much happier than the mood. Arael was sitting on his bed, staring at the wall ahead of him, while he rested his arms and chin on top of his knees. It was lonely in the castle now... The Pneumati had taken more than half of the students, including the other boys that had stayed in Arael's room. Orias was lying under his own bed, holding Nerida close. He'd been hiding there since they got back, and a Coco had been bringing him food. Arael had nothing to do except sketch. The most recent pages of his journal were full of sketches of Virgil.

Nobody was allowed to leave the castle. Nobody was even allowed to go outside. Only the knights if they were accompanied by at least one elder knight. Even then, it was a low chance that they'd let them go outside... Not even Enzo was allowed out unless he was instructed to. Enzo was being watched by Adonis, under the orders of Ariese. It made no sense that they trusted that jerk more than Enzo; all Enzo wanted to do was save the kids who had been taken.

There was a knock on the door that caused Arael to turn his head. It was probably the first time he'd moved in a few hours. "Come in," he said. The door opened up and then Ego walked in. She went straight to Arael's bed and sat down on the end.

"So..." She said. "How's it going?"

Arael simply shrugged. Everyone was quite depressed... They didn't have a clue regarding what to do. They didn't even know where to go to find the stolen kids.

"Have you gotten any of those Dreamwalker vision things?" Ego asked.

Arael shook his head no.

"Well, did you try?"

"They just come to me randomly, there's no try," Arael said.

"…Are you angry with Virgil?"

"Stop cross-examining me…"

"Yeah, he's mad…" Orias said from under the bed.

"He didn't do anything to you," Ego said. "No matter what he is. You don't know! You don't know his life!"

"Just stop!" Arael snapped. "I get it! Okay!? Yes, I'm mad that he turned out to be Pneumati, but I'm not mad at him, I'm mad at me. I should've known that this would happen…"

Ego paused and then nodded understandingly. "You should've if you knew how, but you didn't… Maybe you're not getting anymore because you're blocking it out," she said.

"What would you know…? You block everything out," Arael huffed.

Ego bopped Arael on the forehead, causing him to come out of his grumpy ball position. "You're an idiot! I've had to be this way to get through my life! Not everybody's born with a silver spoon in their mouth! At least I know what I'm doing!" She barked. "…You're not the only one with special powers…"

Orias giggled from under the bed, and then Arael shot a glare his way. He wondered what she meant by 'you're not the only one with special powers.' She must've been hiding something all this time, but it didn't look like she was going to tell them about it.

"Alright, fine… What do you suggest I do then?" Arael asked, rubbing his head.

"Try to use your Dreamwalker thing. I know you haven't tried yet. Maybe it could work. If not, then fine. But at least we know you tried."

Orias poked his head out from under his bed and finally decided to emerge. He wanted to help too, and be a part of this. He wanted to see if Arael could do it and maybe save the other kids. He wanted to save Virgil too; he loved Virgil like an older brother.

Arael stared at Ego and did his best to 'try.' He wasn't even sure how to try. He pursed his lips awkwardly, and sighed in annoyance. "I don't know how…" He said.

"Try lying down and relax," Orias said, pushing Arael down until his head was on the pillow.

Arael looked at Orias in annoyance but decided to play along. He took a breath to try and relax, and then closed his eyes.

"Think about somebody that you know is there, like Virgil. I'm sure his mind would be easy for you to find, since you've been in it before with the nightmares and nonsense," Ego said.

"Okay," Arael said.

He tried focusing on Virgil and the visions that he had about him before. He remembered when he told him that he had to trust him, and the vision of him as a Pneumati.

CHAPTER TWENTY FOUR
Sweet Child of Death

Virgil walked through the swampy nightmare of Blightmire. He'd escaped his room, as he normally would. There was no room that the Pneumati could keep him in that he couldn't get out of. They most likely knew that he was out, but they had no reason to come for him at the moment. He had no shoes on, since the wet rancid ground would've just ruined them anyway, and his clothing was a mess. The symbol of Leodegance that was on his chest was torn away, leaving the black shirt that he wore under it. He had cuts and bruises all over him, and his face was dirty and bloody…

Virgil came to a pool of murky water and crouched down to look at it. He could see his reflection and he wasn't quite happy with it. What a mess… His reflection was dispersed when a four eyed fish jumped out at him and fell back into the water. Everything here was an abomination... Virgil looked over his shoulder after hearing some chatter behind him, and then he quickly took off running so that he wouldn't have to go back to the Pneumati castle. The slimy mud squished between his toes with every step, making a nasty sound that he really didn't care for. He headed to the area that he called 'the cage place,' where the Pneumati kept live kids.

Virgil made it his job to visit the caged ones. He couldn't let them out though, because the Pneumati killed escapees. He was never allowed to learn the Defugio spell, because Ocharos knew that he would use it to help them escape. He wasn't allowed to learn healing magic either, so that he and the kids had to bear the pain of their injuries for punishment. The true evil of the Pneumati couldn't really be known, unless one experienced what happens in the Blightmire swamp...

The cages that the kids were inside of were made out of sticks and bones, but they were enchanted so that they couldn't escape. It was always a terrible sight... Virgil knew that they were safe for the time being though, as long as they didn't do anything to get themselves hurt. The Pneumati always had a set time for when they did what they did with them. What the Pneumati did with the kids was horribly familiar to Virgil. The Pneumati threw them into the marrow pits one by one; if they died in the pits, then they became part of their dark essence to keep the evil magic alive, and if they came out as mindless Pneumati drones, then they were added to the army to keep the Pneumati strong. When the Pneumati took them away, one thing was for sure: they would never been seen again. They only ever used kids, because their will was not strong enough to resist the darkness. Their minds were weakest in the ages of twelve to nineteen, because that was when they were left open to the things that molded them into who they were. With the gates of their minds left wide open, it was easy for the Pneumati to take them away.

Virgil was always the one to take care of the caged kids... When he thought about this, a wave of panic washed over him. What was happening to them while he was gone? Did they suffer more? He felt guilty for leaving them, but he couldn't stand that place any longer. If he just stayed there, then the torture would continue for everyone. There was no way that he could escape Blightmire now though, they'd certainly find him... He needed help.

Virgil walked through the cage place and visited the kids, trying to comfort them as best as he could. There was a calming, yet haunting song spell that he always sang to put them in a sleep-like state for a few hours. It spared them the days of anxiety and terror that they had to endure. That was something that he learned from his mother. She wasn't dead, but she wasn't around either. Virgil didn't quite understand where she went, or why she left him.

Once Virgil was done singing, he checked the kids once more to make sure they were all okay. Next, he went off to find a quiet place in the middle of a cluster of trees. There was a big rock there that was nice to sit on, and the trees blocked out the ugly landscape. When Virgil found the rock, he climbed up on top of it and sat down. There were some charcoal pieces up there that he could use to write on the rocks. It was something to do every once in a while, though he didn't feel like doing much of anything this day, he was exhausted. Ocharos hadn't let him sleep for the past few days. He wasn't as used to it anymore since he was able to sleep without interruption back at Mountainglaive...

Virgil smiled down at a little wooden sculpture sitting on the rock. The sculpture looked like him and somebody else; the other person's face was left unfinished. Virgil rested his back against part of the rock and brought his knees to his chest. He wrapped his arms around his knees and set his chin comfortably on top of them.

He listened to the silence until he began to nod off. Once Virgil was asleep, he immediately started to have a nightmare, but he didn't get too far into it before he felt an odd presence. He'd never felt a presence like this before. His nightmares were always lonely and horrifying, but the new presence was comforting and familiar. Virgil suddenly woke up and looked around.

"Wait! Wait! Go back! That was Arael's presence..." He told himself.

He closed his eyes and tried to sleep again, but it wasn't that easy. He could feel that Arael was still there, he just had to get ahold of him before he slipped away. Virgil quickly switched to a meditative position and tried to relax. He closed his eyes and breathed a spell that could help him get into his own head again. If he could go into a sleeping state where he was still conscious of himself, then he could tell Arael where he was!

Virgil sat there for a moment, continuing to whisper the spell over and over again until it finally worked. It was all about timing, but saying it over and over again made his chances of making it work much higher. Virgil went into his own head, appearing in a completely different nightmare than the last one. He payed attention to what his dream self was doing, trying to control it, as he felt Arael's presence come back. Arael's added presence made it easier for Virgil to take control of his dream self, which was a difficult task that took an immense amount of concentration.

"Arael?" Virgil said. His voice sounded warped, and it was like three of him were talking at once.

He was speaking in the real world too, so he had to be careful not to be too loud, in order to avoid drawing the attention of the Pneumati. The nightmare world looked like a huge, flat desert with a black sandstorm blowing around. The sand under his feet was dark grey, and the sky was a faded purple. The wind was chaotic, changing direction at random. Virgil looked around and then took a step, which caused a colossal, dead banyan tree to suddenly emerge from the sand. The tree was so big that it unexpectedly grew from the ground under Virgil and knocked him down, scratching him with its branches as it stretched up into the sky. It almost made him lose the focus that he had on his dream self. Once Virgil was clear of the branches, he got up off of the ground and looked at his wounds. His blood turned into dark sludge and began turning him into something else; his pure Pneumati self that he hoped he would never have to see.

"It's not real, it's not real," Virgil told himself, making his dream self suddenly go back to normal. "Arael? Are you there?"

Virgil turned around and suddenly saw Arael. He was just standing there, having no way of controlling himself in these dreams yet. Arael was just a spectator in this, so Virgil had to do all of the work. He ran to Arael and grabbed his shoulders. "You're here!" He said. "Please don't leave. I know you're mad, but you have to trust me!"

Arael had no reaction and just continued to stare off into nowhere.

"Listen, I'm in a place called Blightmire. It's completely forbidden to come here, but if you told the Chancellor, then maybe she'd listen. She already knew that I was Pneumati... All of the kids are here!" Virgil said.

He paused when he suddenly heard a ruckus going on in the real world. His body jerked in panic and woke him up, taking his mind back to the rock that he was sitting on. Virgil's eyes quickly darted around, finding nothing, and then he closed his eyes and pushed himself back into the nightmare before he lost it.

Arael was still there, and Virgil had to find out how to tell him where exactly Blightmire was... In a split second though, Arael had disappeared from his position. When Virgil looked around, he saw that the banyan tree was gone, and he was in Blightmire swamp. There were absent minded Pneumati all around, but they weren't going to do anything. They were like dressmaker's dummies. Virgil glanced around and spotted Arael once again. He was standing near one of the white pools, with his feet sinking into the mud. Virgil tried to call for him, but he found that he couldn't speak now... It was because he was afraid of being heard, he was sure of that... The mind was a powerful thing, playing along with one's fears and emotions. He had to find another way to talk to Arael now.

Virgil ran to Arael's side and quickly got an idea. He grabbed Arael's head and turned it toward the mud, before quickly writing on the ground, with his finger. He started to hear more commotion going on in the real world, so he rushed his task. When he was done, he moved out of the way so that Arael could see the mud. He'd drawn a map; a map from Mauntainglaive to Blightmire. He hoped that it was good enough for him to use. Blightmire was far away from Mountainglave, it was all the way on the other side of Domhan. Virgil could hear somebody coming to his real world body and it was terrifying. He looked up at Arael in panic, just as Arael suddenly had a reaction. His head turned and he was about to say something, but then Virgil was pulled out of his sleep state.

Virgil screamed and kicked, returning back to the real world as his brother, Malachi yanked him down from the rock that he was sitting on.

"There you are! Hiding from us! You didn't believe that you had permission to get comfortable yet, did you? You haven't earned that quite yet!" Malachi said, grabbing Virgil by the hair and dragging him with him.

"Let go of me!" Virgil yelled, pushing Malachi away and trying to run.

That was something that he never tried to do, but the adrenaline that was pumping through his veins wanted to deviate a bit.

"What is the matter with you!? You're such a brat!" Malachi laughed before tossing a spell toward Virgil's head, knocking him senseless.

CHAPTER TWENTY FIVE
Realization

Arael suddenly sat up and gasped in surprise. He quickly looked between Orias and Ego, who were staring at him eagerly.

"Did you do it!? Did it work!?" Ego asked.

Arael's eyes started watering as he remembered the ugly scenes in Virgil's nightmare, and the way that he looked at him before he was taken away. Arael didn't know who or what had ended the nightmare, but he didn't like it, and it made him feel a sense of urgency to find this place.

"I- I did!" Arael squeaked. "The way he looked at me- I'm so sorry..." Arael buried his face in his hands to let out a few tears.

"Who!?" Orias asked.

Arael looked up and wiped his nose. "It was Virgil. He drew me a map!"

He quickly started to look around and go through his stuff, until he found his journal and charcoal pencil, which he'd forgotten were right next to him. Next, he jotted down the map as best as he could, trying to get every detail that he could remember onto the page. When he was done, he tossed it in front of Ego and Orias for them to see.

"What on Domhan...?" Ego said, looking at the map in confusion. "I don't think anything exists there."

"Wait!" Orias said, grabbing the journal to see the map. "I know this place!"

"Blightmire..." Arael said.

"Yeah!" Orias yelled. "Blightmire!"

"Don't even say that! Arael, do you even know how forbidden it is to go to... The bad place!?" Ego said.

"Yes. But what else are we supposed to do?" Arael asked. "Virgil was literally begging for help."

"...I like the way you think... But we can't just run in there head first. That's something I do a lot and always regret," Ego said. "I'm sure we'd all rather not die."

Orias grabbed Ego's hand and yanked on it. "Come on! Let's get Enzo!" He yelled, before yanking on Arael's hand too, and dashing out of the room.

CHAPTER TWENTY SIX

As Good as Dead

It had been four more days since Virgil had contacted Arael through his nightmare. Virgil hoped that Arael listened to his call for help, but he knew that Arael didn't like him. Arael probably wanted him dead now. How could he have ever believed that anyone would accept him for who he really was? He didn't even truly accept himself. He'd been working to fight who he was all his life, but maybe he just couldn't fight it anymore... Maybe he was destined to be who Ocharos wanted him to be.

All his life, he'd been a disappointment. Nothing he ever did was good enough. It was always what his father wanted. Virgil didn't want that though... He didn't want to submit to the evil that he was born into. Really, he would rather die than fulfill his birthright... Maybe he was selfish... Maybe he was wise... One thing was for sure, he felt that fighting this was the only right thing to do.

Zillah pounded on the wall next to Virgil's head angrily, but he didn't flinch. He stayed still, completely void of emotion. Not a thing that the Pneumati were doing was going to get the location of Mountainglaive out of him. Even though they all hated him, he was content with knowing that he saved the rest of the kids from these horrendous acts. His siblings had taken him to an old, burned cottage that was placed near the edge of the swamp. It was to keep the noise at a minimum, because Ocharos was asleep in his castle of dead trees, although the distant sounds of screams were soothing to the vile creature.

"You'll tell me now!" Zillah screamed at Virgil impatiently.

Virgil stayed silent, with his hands and feet bound to the wall with rusted chains. Malachi entered the room and stared at Virgil with crossed arms.

"We always knew that he's not the easiest to get words out of... But it's never been like this..." Malachi said.

It was true. Virgil rarely ever spoke. He probably spoke more words back at Mountainglaive than he ever did in his entire life.

"Stubborn brat!" Zillah growled.

Virgil followed their every movement with cold eyes, refusing to say a word. Even though he felt broken of emotion, in his heart he was still angry. It was the only thing fueling him at this point.

"We can't necessarily kill him and he knows it! We've already tried that before anyway, and it never did anything..." Zillah yelled.

Virgil continued to stare. He decided to try something, subtly uttering the words to the Fluttari Motis spell. Metal began to clink against objects behind Malachi, but Malachi ignored the noise. Suddenly, a knife flew out from a pile of stolen goods, heading straight for Malachi's head. Quickly, Malachi caught the knife between his fingers and then he casually examined it.

"Nice try, brat," Malachi said as he slowly walked to Virgil and pressed the cold metal blade against the teen's face. "You think that you're powerful. But you'll never be as powerful as father. I don't even understand why he hasn't disposed of you yet." Malachi dragged the knife across Virgil's face, causing blood to drip from a cut that it had left behind. Virgil stayed silent with no reaction to the fresh wound on his face. That pain meant nothing to him. "What if we kill your friends? Slowly tear their flesh from their little bodies? If you tell us where the others are, then we'll spare them the pain."

"Yes, that's what we'll do! Those kids mean nothing to us! They'll die like ants beneath our feet!" Zillah agreed.

They waited for a reaction from Virgil, but to their surprise, he only let out a smug little grin, as if he were mocking them. That was certainly new. Their brother was different from before he ran away, and they didn't like it, not one bit.

"You think this is funny!?" Zillah yelled, as she tossed a knife into the wall, just missing Virgil's face.

"I don't believe that he actually cares about those infections. Nor do they care for him. You saw their faces when they saw what he really is," said Malachi.

"Doubt it," Zillah replied as she turned her attention back to Virgil. "Big brother, Virgee…" She said in a sweet voice. "If you don't tell us where the kids are, like you were supposed to do in the first place, I'm afraid that father is going to have to punish the world greatly for these troubles. And I'm sure you know that you'll have to be punished by torture for the rest of your insignificant life."

Once again, they got absolutely no reaction from Virgil. Zillah screamed in anger, pounding her fists against the walls and kicking objects across the room. It used to be so easy to get things out of him! He'd be hesitant to speak, but he never took this much beating!

"We've tried everything! He just won't break!" She yelled. "What is happening to you, brother? Why do you betray us!?"

Malachi stood in front of Virgil for a moment, looking him over as he thought about what to do. "Do you remember that trick that I've been learning?" He asked.

"Yes…" Zillah grumbled, pounding her head against the wall.

"…I know what we can do," Malachi smirked at Virgil menacingly, believing that there was no possible way that his new idea could fail. It never failed in the history of dark magic, and it was reluctant to break its winning streak.

"What?" Zillah asked.

"Remember the technique that was used on King Ottimo years ago? When the Pneumati were unable to kill him because of some information he withheld, but we used this trick to get him to spill all of his secrets?"

Zillah looked at Malachi with wide eyes. "Yes! Can we do that!?"

They finally got a small reaction out of Virgil, as his eyes slightly shifted in fear. He'd learned about this 'trick' in Lady Agnes's class. It was a horrible thing that the Pneumati had invented. He knew about this before, but never really thought of it much until he learned more about what his father was actually doing with it.

Malachi held his hand out in front of himself as dark, Pneumati magic began to float above his large hand. The magic began to move almost as if it were a living creature while Malachi and Zillah stared at it with evil, toothy grins. Malachi closed his fingers around the magic and brought his hand to Virgil's face. Virgil turned his head away, as sweat began to drip down his forehead.

"Now, you're scared. Good," Malachi said, putting his fist to Virgil's mouth. Virgil closed his lips tightly, trying not to let the magic enter his body, but Malachi grabbed his jaw with his free hand, violently forcing it open. "Now, tell us where the castle is, brother."

Malachi slid the black, animal-like energy into Virgil's mouth and pressed his palm over his lips to prevent it from escaping. Once the evil magic crawled down

Virgil's throat, Malachi removed his hand from his face and smiled maniacally. Virgil gasped as he looked at the floor with wide eyes, letting out a few squeaks of fear with his breath. Zillah and Malachi watched and waited for the magic to take its effect... Virgil tried to keep his breathing steady, as sweat dripped down his face and off of his nose, falling to the floor drop by drop. He knew exactly what to expect, but it was terrifying nonetheless.

"He'll have to talk now," Malachi smirked.

Virgil let out a slight pained whine as the magic began to take its effect on the inside of his body, but he still refused to say a word. He squeezed his eyes shut tightly as his body began to violently convulse. His stomach contracted, his muscles tightened and burned and his back felt as though there were a million needles penetrating his flesh; he tried to hold in a scream, but he just couldn't.

"Tell us now or this will only get worse for you," Malachi said.

Despite the intense pain, Virgil still refused to tell them anything, letting himself be tortured for as long as it would take. He was used to it anyway, his father was never once good to him and if he told these two anything, it still wouldn't change his fate; he knew how they were. The people who he had considered to be his friends didn't even care about him anymore. He was born to be a monster. Nobody would be hurt if they ended up killing him, right...?

This went on for an hour, causing the two Pneumati to grow even more impatient.

"He has a strong will..." Zillah said, twisting her pinky around in her ear as they listened to their brother's screams of pain.

"We still have another option," Malachi said as he began conjuring another spell, the same as the one before.

Malachi stood in front of Virgil once more, with the violent magic floating above his hand.

"No! No!" Virgil cried loudly, finally saying something to them.

"Nope, you'll have to tell me where the castle is if you want it to be over," Malachi smiled, like he was butchering a simple hog.

Virgil just cried, so Malachi finished conjuring the spell.

"Please stop!" Virgil screamed desperately, with tears flowing down his cheeks.

Virgil screamed even louder as Malachi let the magic enter his body again.

"I can't breathe!" Virgil gasped.

"Poor baby," Zillah said, walking to him. "Will you tell us now?"

Virgil shook his head no, barely getting words out, "No! Never again! Never again!"

Zillah went to his side and hugged him, resting her head against his, even while he was thrashing around. She started petting his hair with her cold hand, ready for him to talk. "It'll all be over when you just give us what we want. Poor, poor brother..." She hummed.

Unexpectedly, the door busted open and launched all the way across the room of the burned cottage, breaking it to pieces. Malachi glanced at the entrance and quickly cast Defugio to escape, leaving Virgil and Zillah behind without a second thought. A blue discharge of magic came through the doorway and hit Zillah, causing her to shriek as it burned her skin. It was an Aegis spell! She looked to Virgil and then to the doorway, where she saw that she was now outnumbered, so she quickly cast Defugio, just as another Aegis blast was sent her way.

Lady Agnes and Sir Enzo suddenly stormed into the room, with Arael, Ego and Orias behind them. Lady Agnes blasted the restraints off of Virgil, setting him free, while Enzo caught him and lowered him to the floor. Virgil was still crying, for the bad magic was still inside of him.

"What's wrong with him!?" Ego asked in panic.

"Oh, dear goodness!" Lady Agnes said, rushing to Virgil's side and taking his head in her arms.

She waved her hand over the teen's mouth, causing him to gag and puke up what looked like an enormous, slimy black leech. The leech writhed on the ground for a moment and then burned away, but Virgil still hadn't stopped struggling. His body jolted away from her, and he fell on his side, curling up and gripping his stomach.

"There's- another," Virgil struggled to say, with barely enough air in his lungs to even breath.

Lady Agnes took his head in her arms again and made him dry heave a few times before the remaining leech-like creature finally escaped from his body. Virgil gasped for air as the horrible experience finally stopped, and he cried tears of relief. Arael ran to his side and kneeled down next to him to see if he was okay. When Virgil opened his eyes enough to see the people around him, he felt so much happiness, especially when he saw Arael. To Arael's surprise, Virgil quickly sat up and grabbed him in a tight hug, to cry on his chest. "You came! You finally came!" He bawled.

Before Arael could say anything, Enzo urged them to get up. "Come now, we have to leave quickly!" He said. They were still in Pneumati territory after all.

Arael nodded silently, while Enzo grabbed Virgil's arm to try and help him up. The boy didn't want to let go of his friend, so it took a bit of effort to get him off. Virgil was still upset; he must have been in a state of shock after all of that. He couldn't move well either. His whole body ached and felt so weak, but Enzo yanked him up despite this. They were all going to be in a world of pain if they were caught.

"Son, you have to help us find the stolen kids!" Enzo said, trying to snap Virgil out of it.

Virgil coughed and shook his head, getting some of his senses back. "Come on," he said, bringing Enzo out the door.

The others followed cautiously, none of them could believe what they were doing. They were forbidden to be here, but they had to help anyway… It was difficult enough to get away from Mountainglaive without getting caught by the legion masters, who had been keeping a close eye on everything. Once they got to the cage place, Virgil stopped them all and pointed toward it. There were Pneumati patrolling the area, but there weren't very many. Most of the Pneumati were normally sleeping in the Marrow Pits, so it was quiet. That didn't mean that they couldn't hear their uninvited guests though... They could come out at the slightest sound of a breath.

As they examined the area, Enzo and Lady Agnes looked concerned. It was obvious why though... There were many, many kids all caged up. It was going to be near impossible to get them all out safely. Even then, Lady Agnes wouldn't be able to cast Defugio on them all in time. If they did it only a few at a time, they still would be caught. The kids were still under Virgil's spell too, so he had to get them out of it, or else they would never be able to run.

"I can get them," Virgil said, still weak.

Virgil pushed himself away from Enzo and started stumbling into the cage place. Arael took a step forward to chase after him, but Ego stopped him. They didn't realize that the Pneumati didn't care about Virgil's presence. Arael had almost forgotten that he had just found out what Virgil really was. Lady Agnes and Enzo, however, were quite surprised. They didn't truly believe the story until now.

Virgil looked around at the few Pneumati surrounding him, and quietly began waking up the kids with a reverse to his spell. They began to stir, noticing where they were once again. Toward the end of the cage place, Virgil tripped and fell into the mud. The others weren't sure if they should go and get him or not... From the ground, Virgil cast a spell that caused too much commotion for comfort. "Fluttari Motis!" All of the cages opened at the same time, allowing the kids to escape. Virgil stayed in the mud, trying to get up. He didn't want anybody to be left behind, but he wasn't going to be able to do anything about it.

The Pneumati immediately noticed what was going on and lunged toward the sight. In panic, Lady Agnes quickly started casting Defugio on as many kids as she could. Some of them ran off, into the woods or in the complete opposite direction. Arael had lost sight of Virgil in the panicking crowd now. On instinct, he ran into the mass of fleeing kids to find him. On the way, he ran into a Pneumati and quickly cut it down into smelly black mush. It was terrifying to be in this place. No human being should've been there. No living being should've been there.

"Virgil!" Arael called, glancing around and pushing passed the kids. Arael spun around on his heels and finally spotted Virgil. He was still lying in the mud, so Arael dashed to him and grabbed his arm, slipping to a stop. "Come on, Virgil! Get up!" He said.

Despite their efforts, there was no way that Arael was going to get him up, so he tried to drag him.

"Help everyone else first!" Virgil demanded.

"We can't!" Arael said.

The Pneumati were beginning to swoop in and grab armfuls of kids, to get them back into their cages. Virgil wanted them all to be saved, but the Pneumati were gathering them up too quickly. Arael looked up and saw a Pneumati that was different than the other ones. This one had to be at least seven feet tall! It just stood there, near one of the pits of white liquid. Virgil turned and saw it too. Ocharos had noticed the disturbance, and he now saw Arael as well. Ocharos glared at the two boys with his devilish eyes. He didn't attempt to do anything; all that he did was stare.

Enzo ran through the crowd, accidentally getting clipped in the side by one of the Pneumati. Enzo struck it down with Aegis, and then he picked up Virgil and swung him over his shoulder. "Come! We must leave!" Enzo said, running back toward the others as Arael followed.

"Wait! Save them!" Virgil yelled, staring at the kids that were being scooped back into confinement.

Arael and Enzo didn't listen and just kept running. They were getting further and further away from the kids. How could they just leave them!?

"Go back!" Virgil yelled, slamming his fist into Enzo's back. "They're going to die!"

Virgil saw the child that had spoken to him when they had first arrived there. The child screamed his name as he was scooped up by Virgil's very own twin brother. The child was terrified! He reached his hands out toward him, desperate for help. Virgil stared between his brother and the child in horror. Malachi watched Virgil being taken away as he held onto the panicking child. He stood there and just smiled, before gently grabbing the child's head.

"Malachi! Malachi, don't!" Virgil shouted.

Malachi didn't care. With a swift jerk of the head, the child was gone, and his essence flowed from his body to power the Pneumati that killed him... Malachi smiled even wider at Virgil, with no care for the kids. He had no heart. His only mission was to torture and gain power.

"No!" Virgil wailed, as Malachi disappeared from sight when Lady Agnes cast Defugio.

In a moment, Enzo, Arael, Orias, Ego, Lady Agnes and Virgil were all in the field behind Mountainglaive, along with the kids that they were able to save. Hammurabi was waiting there for them, so he quickly started to tend to everyone's injuries. Enzo put Virgil down on the ground, but the boy suddenly became quiet. No matter what they said to him, he wouldn't respond. Hammurabi took everyone to the infirmary for the night, to watch over them. Most of the kids were still horrified, while others seemed to be okay. It was no secret now that the rescue party had broken some rules, so the legion masters pulled them aside to speak with them... They may have caused more conflict than there was already, but at least some of the kids were safe. The legion masters felt that it was a crime to bring the son of Ocharos back to this place...

CHAPTER TWENTY SEVEN
Prosecution

"That was quite uncalled for…" Said Enzo.

The rescue party was making its way back to Hammurabi's infirmary after speaking to the legion masters. The legion masters were beyond angry with them, but Enzo and the others were able to convince the legion masters to let Virgil speak, before they decided what they were going to do with him. Enzo was in the biggest trouble, but he didn't care… Arael was angry with the legion masters for what they were doing. Now the castle was under an even tighter lockdown. It was like they didn't want the other kids to be saved at all. The truth was that even though the legion masters were said to be all powerful and all knowing, they were cowards, and they had been in charge for far too long.

"What's going to happen?" Orias asked. "I don't understand why they're being like this!"

"I don't know, but it took every bone in my body not to give them a piece of my mind!" Ego growled.

"I feel bad for the other kids. They have to let us go back for them!" Orias said.

"Well, that's not a choice that we have any power over at the moment, I'm afraid," Enzo said.

"I just don't understand them…" Arael said. "Those kids were their students… They're just going to let them die there?"

"Why isn't the Chancellor doing anything about it!?" Ego asked.

"She's trying, believe me," Enzo said. "She provided cover for us while we were away, and she'll continue to do what she thinks is best."

They all entered the infirmary, where Hammurabi was sitting in a chair, reading his book as always. There were some kids sleeping in the beds, but they were okay. None of them were seriously injured, just rattled.

Hammurabi put his book down and stood up to greet them. "Well? What happened?" He asked.

"They're not being very cooperative, but we bought some time," Enzo answered.

Hammurabi nodded and looked to Ego, Orias and Arael. "Your friend is over there," he pointed to a lonely bed in the corner, where Virgil was laying. "I fixed him up, but he still won't talk to me."

They all walked to the lonely bed to see Virgil. They didn't expect him to be awake, but he was. He was just lying there, staring at a fixed point somewhere in the room. His hands were shaking, and he looked more pale and sick than he usually did. Arael pulled up a chair and sat next to him, while Orias sat on the floor and Ego stood nearby.

"What are we to do, Rabi…" Enzo said, shaking his head.

Hammurabi looked Enzo over and pushed him down onto a chair. "I will tell you what we can do now, is put you back together," he said, pointing to the wound in his side.

Enzo didn't fight him, instead he took his heavy chest plate off. He was hit in a vulnerable place between his chest and back plates, and the leather straps between the two were cut now. The Pneumati that clipped him in the side, actually got him pretty good, and the dark magic was starting to set in to the wound; Hammurabi knew how to get rid of it though, that was one of his specialties as a healer. Hammurabi went to work on Enzo's wound, while the others stayed where they were. Orias leaned his back up against the bed that Virgil was lying in while petting Nerida, and Ego stared at the floor silently, with her arms crossed. They all felt a bit betrayed in more than one way…

Arael leaned in and placed his hand over Virgil's shaking hand. It felt very cold. Arael hadn't touched his bare hands before, but this must've been how they always were. Arael sighed, "Listen… I know that you're upset. I know you've been through a lot, and I'm sorry. I'm sorry for the way I treated you. I'm sorry that I burned you. I'm sorry about everything…" He paused. "The legion masters don't want you to stay here… We made sure that they would give you a chance first though. So if you really want to stay here, you have to convince them somehow… It's true that I am disappointed about what you turned out to be, but after everything, you've earned my trust, and I will not ever leave your side."

Arael looked at him in silence, receiving no reply. He knew that Virgil was listening though; his eyes were full of tears. Arael thought for a moment, and then pulled the piece of Aegis crystal that Virgil had given him out of the collar of his shirt. "I kept this. I even made a necklace out of it. It helps me a lot every day…" He said. "We found your swallow wand, but it was broken. I saved your Aegis crystal. It's in the crate next to my bed."

Once again, the only reply from Virgil was silence…

Orias stood up and put Nerida on Virgil's side, to let her lay on him and sniff him like a puppy. "Here, Virgil. Nerida helps me when I'm sad. Maybe she can help you too," he smiled.

"What are we supposed to do when he has to stand before the legion masters? If he's brain dead like this and won't say anything to defend himself, then they're going to get rid of him for sure," Ego said, insensitively. "They want him in five minutes!"

"…I don't know…" Arael said.

The tears in Virgil's eyes started to run down his face, and his hands continued to shake. His whole body was shivering. Arael felt his fingers ball up into a fist under his hand. Maybe he was just lost at words… There was no way that he was just going to let himself be tossed away by the legion masters; he was too stubborn for that.

Arael only hoped that Virgil would know what he was doing like always.

"Oh, I wouldn't push him too hard right now. That spell that Lady Agnes told me the Pneumati put in him was quite horrid. I would expect that anybody would respond this way…" Hammurabi said.

Arael shook his head. "No… He's okay."

Just then, Sir Gwenael came to the doorway and knocked on the wall. "Excuse me… The legion masters… They're ready," he said.

Everyone looked at Sir Gwenael and then stood up to leave.

"This isn't fair!" Ego shouted.

"I know it isn't," said Enzo. "We need to have trust… Fruke always says that everything happens for a reason, and I trust in that."

"Yeah, but a good reason or a bad reason?" Ego asked rudely.

"…Good luck then," Hammurabi said.

Enzo smiled at Hammurabi and got ready to go. Arael grabbed Virgil's shoulder to help him up, but then Virgil suddenly picked up Nerida and handed her to Orias before getting up by himself. He still wasn't looking at anybody or planning on saying anything. Everyone looked at each other and then started walking, making their way to the vestibule. Virgil followed Enzo without a problem, while Arael followed behind him and the other two behind Arael. Enzo and the others were going to have to stand with Virgil too, since they were the ones who brought him back, although they weren't allowed to say anything... It wasn't fair at all.

When they came to the vestibule, all of the elder knights and the remaining legions were waiting there. The legion masters were all sitting up high, like they were some kind of special. They thought much too highly of themselves... Most of them fled during the chaos of their own choosing ceremony. Nobody in their right mind would've expressed such cowardice. Schlimm was sitting with them, with a smug look on his face. Arael wondered why Enzo and the elder knights weren't in the place of the legion masters. They were much better people, and they fought until the end. Even the Chancellor was there. She looked very upset with all of this, and she looked at Enzo like she wanted to slap him then hug him immediately afterwards.

Virgil stopped in the middle of the room and looked up at the legion masters, while the others stood near him. They all were standing respectfully, even though the legion masters didn't deserve the respect... Ariese stood up first. Arael found out that Ariese was the leader of everything. All of this. All of these people. Even him. Ariese was not a good man in anyone's eyes now.

"Virgil Capello..." Ariese started. "If that is even your real name, lying, Pneumati filth!" His words were harsh, and full of hate. It was clear that Ariese had already made his decision on what he wanted to do with Virgil...

Arael wanted to yell at Ariese for that. His whole body ached with frustration, but if he said anything, it would only make things worse. The others felt the same… He couldn't even imagine how angry Ego felt, since she wasn't one to hold in her rage. Virgil tilted his head at Ariese and smiled at him. It wasn't a nice smile though; it was a furious smile. Like that smile that you get from people who are just completely fed up; that unsettling smile of somebody who is trying to keep themselves together so they won't strangle you.

"Yes sir, that is my real name… Virgil is the name that Ocharos gave to me, and Capello was my mother's surname…" He said. "I never hid that."

"Silence!" Ariese yelled. "Do you realize that if you do not prove your worth to us here and now, you are to be executed!?"

Executed!? That wasn't supposed to be part of this!? Arael took a step forward in concern, but Enzo held him back. This didn't make any sense! They told them before that they were only going to have him exiled, not executed! It couldn't have been a misunderstanding or a slip of the tongue, Ariese had to have just now decided this.

This time, Virgil frowned at Ariese before he spoke, "Yes sir…"

"Good…" Ariese growled. "Now… Do you deny the fact that you are of Pneumati blood?"

"No sir," Virgil said.

"Do you deny that you have used dark magic, even with the knowledge that it is forbidden?"

"No sir."

"Then why do you believe that you should not be executed?"

Virgil paused for a moment and smiled again, while everyone waited in suspense for what he was going to say. "Were the many children who were wrongfully stolen by the Pneumati evil?" He asked.

Everyone looked at Virgil in confusion. "What?" Ariese asked.

"Were the children evil, before they were transformed into Pneumati puppets, for Ocharos's army? Or turned to mush to power them?" Virgil repeated, in more detail.

"No, boy," Leodegrance answered this time.

"Then why do you not blame them?" Virgil asked. "They've killed many. I've killed none."

"Because they were not born to be Pneumati!" Ariese roared.

"But nobody is Pneumati before they are turned! I am not one of them!" Virgil snapped.

Arael stared between the legion masters and Virgil, afraid of what they were going to do. He'd never felt so much built up anxiety in his life.

"But you are!" Ariese argued.

"No! I have worked my entire life to make sure I did not fulfill what I was born to be! If anything, I have weakened the Pneumati! Because you know why!? I'm meant to be Ocharos, the one you've called Dieudonne! I'm meant to do worse than he ever could after he dies! I am his son, built for unspeakable things!" Virgil yelled.

"You dare raise your voice to me!?" Ariese boomed.

"Yes, I dare! I've earned it! I've let myself be tortured and beaten for my entire life, because I don't want to see this world destroyed! I want the Pneumati to burn in the deepest pits of hell! I tried to save the kids from the Pneumati when nobody ever came! Is this how you repay me!?" Virgil snapped. "I thought that there was something left in this world that was worth saving, but maybe I was wrong!"

Ariese looked at Virgil in astonishment, but it wasn't good astonishment... "That is it! You are to be executed at sundown! My decision is final!" He roared.

The room went completely silent... Arael glanced around in panic; he didn't know what to do about any of this! If anything, he was going to help Virgil escape before sundown. That was all that he could come up with on the spot. Virgil was looking down at the floor, obviously crying. This wasn't good at all! What on Domhan were the legion masters thinking!

"Maybe..." Virgil started. "Maybe, I should've spared myself the years of pain and let Ocharos make me into his own image..." He paused. "But then again... I wouldn't be any better than you people... You could've saved those kids, but you didn't... You never did after all these years, you never even tried..."

Next, Virgil stepped toward Arael and put his cold hand on his cheek. Arael found himself leaning his head into the boy's hand once it was there, seeking comfort. Arael wasn't sure what was going on now. He didn't even know what Virgil was doing, until Virgil looked at him.   It wasn't threatening at all, more warm and welcoming.

"Show them, Arael. Please, show them," Virgil said.

Arael knew what he meant now. He had to do what he did when he found Virgil through his nightmare. Arael nodded and then closed his eyes. The legion masters jumped up, intending to attack Virgil before he could do anything, but time seemed to have stopped altogether.

CHAPTER TWENTY EIGHT
Welcome to My World

The nightmare started in the middle of Blightmire swamp… Only, it wasn't quite a nightmare this time; it was a memory. With Virgil and Arael's combined efforts, they were able to make memories once again real, and bring it to the minds of everyone in the vestibule. This memory was from only a year ago, just before Virgil ran away from the swamp. He looked a lot different in the memory, and he had to have been Arael's age. Both of his eyes were the same, instead of one being scarred, and there was more color in his whole being; he looked alive with olive toned skin, and light brown hair.

Virgil was running through the swamp barefoot, wearing the same tattered clothing that he'd arrived at Mountainglaive in. Once Virgil stopped, he saw the army of Pneumati returning from one of their raids. They had riches and food, and most of all, kids. There were even a few barrels full of a certain drink on the back of the Pneumati's carts that were all too familiar to Arael. To Arael, it appeared that he was following behind Virgil. It had to have been the same for everyone else as well, but he couldn't see them; though, he knew that they were there.

Virgil watched as the Pneumati passed by, with all of the stolen goods. There was a boy that was about his age, crammed into a small box with two others. The boy had black hair, as dark as the night. Arael recognized him almost immediately, from one of the visions that he had; the boy whose face bled after he told someone to promise that they'd end it, whatever 'it' was.

The memory flashed forward to a point where Virgil was walking through the cage place. There, he saw the boy with black hair again. This time, he was in a cage by himself. Virgil approached the cage and sat down next to it. The boy turned to look at him, and then his eyes lit up with hope.

"Who are you?" The boy asked.

"My name's Virgil."

"Are you an angel sent to help us?"

"No," Virgil smiled, "But, I am here to help. I always try to help the kids here."

"Well, you sure look like an angel to me," the boy smiled.

The memory flashed forward again. Virgil and the boy with black hair were out in the dead woods, walking side by side. Virgil must've let the boy out of the cage, even though he was forbidden to do so. Virgil took the boy to the rock that he liked to sit on when he wanted some peace from all of the evil in the swamp.

During the next few flashes forward, the memory showed how Virgil and boy had become good friends. Virgil and the boy always tried to help the other kids escape, but it never worked. Virgil was always able to hide the fact that he was letting his friend out, and that the boy was helping with the attempted escapes. Whenever Ocharos found out about Virgil's independent deviations, he would beat Virgil to the edge of death, and then have Virgil's brother heal him to keep him alive when he couldn't take it anymore.

When Virgil was not with his friend, Ocharos was working him to the bone, training him to the best of his abilities. There was no option except for perfection. Since Virgil was only by minutes the eldest of Ocharos's kin, and born a mage, then it was his destiny to surpass Ocharos and all that he was, to take over as the lord of Pneumati. When Virgil made mistakes, then he was punished. When he refused to do something that Ocharos wanted, he was punished. Arael understood why everything that he ever did was so flawless now...

In the next flash forward, Virgil was sitting on the rock in the woods, with the boy again.

"I don't know what to do... My father is going to try and turn me to one of them tomorrow... Zillah and Malachi have already started, willingly," Virgil said.

"Run away," said the boy.

"Run away?" Virgil repeated.

"Yes. You haven't tried that yet, have you?"

"No, but I can't leave the kids. And if my father found out, then-"

"Then what? He tortures you anyway. How could he do any worse?"

"He could kill all of the kids," Virgil said.

"Virgil, he does anyway... We've tried to stop it, but there's no changing his mind."

"I know... I've never been away from here before. Are you going to come with me?"

"Of course!" The boy said. "We'll run away together, forever. We'll find a way to stop Ocharos once and for all!"

Virgil smiled at the boy and turned his attention to a piece of wood that he was carving into something. He didn't know what it was supposed to be yet, and the boy wouldn't tell him.

"I don't care what 'destiny' says..." The boy said. "You're not a bad person, even if you're not really a person. Just promise me that you won't give up on stopping Ocharos."

Virgil nodded yes. "I promise," he said. "So, we'll run away tomorrow morning? Before the ritual?" Virgil asked.

"Yeah," the boy smiled, carving a familiar face into the piece of wood.

The memory flashed forward once again. Nobody expected what was going to happen next. It was just after Virgil and the boy had attempted to run away, only Malachi caught them in the act and Virgil couldn't lie his way out of it. Malachi told Ocharos about what the two had done, and they were both going to be punished severely for their actions. Not only did they find out that the two were going to run away, but they found out what Virgil had been doing before that – letting the boy out and planning these deeds with him.

Malachi held the boy back, as Ocharos yelled at Virgil and beat him senseless in front of his friend, and all of the other kids. "How dare you!" Ocharos's voice boomed. "How dare you defy your father!?" Ocharos grabbed Virgil's arm and yanked him toward one of the Marrow pits nearby. "You will become my successor, and you will never defy me again, for the darkness will consume your soul and whatever light that you dare hold onto!"

Ocharos pushed Virgil to the edge of the Marrow Pit and stomped on his back. He wanted him to go into the pit, to become nothing but Pneumati, to let go of everything that he'd been fighting for.

"Don't let him do it, Virgil!" Yelled his friend.

Ocharos whirled around and stomped over to the boy that Malachi held, and then slapped him across the face with no hesitation. The slap had so much force behind it that it caused the boy's face to bleed.

Virgil couldn't believe this! "Don't touch him!" He yelled. That was the first time that he had ever raised his voice to Ocharos...

Ocharos slowly turned around and looked at Virgil, with his devilish eyes. "You dare...? After all that I've done for you?" He growled. Ocharos raised his hand to hit the boy again, and then unexpectedly, Virgil jumped up and blasted Aegis his way.

"Aegis!" Virgil yelled. "Aegis, Aegis, Aegis!" He repeated over and over, in so much rage.

The spell burned Ocharos as he stood in front of Malachi to protect him. Ocharos was able to heal almost immediately. The only thing that Virgil managed to do was make him angry.

"You ungrateful little maggot!" Ocharos yelled. "I did not teach you that spell! How dare you use this magic against your own father!? This boy, did he teach Aegis to you!?"

Virgil stopped and stared at Ocharos in a mixture of panic and anger. The boy did teach him Aegis. The boy taught him a lot of things.

"Did he!?" Ocharos repeated even louder.

Virgil shook his head no, before Ocharos turned around and grabbed the boy by the neck.

"Leave him alone! Leave him alone!" Virgil yelled.

Without thought, Ocharos conjured a spell and shot the boy with it, before tossing him at Virgil. The boy hit Virgil at full speed, causing them both to get sent tumbling backwards, to the edge of the Marrow Pit. Virgil quickly recovered from the impact and grabbed his friend, cradling his head in his arms.

"No! No!" Virgil bawled.

The boy's face was bloody, and he was being eaten away by the evil magic, just like when Virgil got hit in the arm, during Enzo's test. The boy was surely dying, and Virgil didn't know how to stop the dark magic. The boy gasped and grabbed onto Virgil's hand, saying those familiar words that Arael remembered from his vision. "Promise you'll end it... Promise you'll stop them!?"

Virgil nodded and hugged his friend closely as he turned to nothing but dust. The boy's soul combined with Virgil; the dead's souls always went to the nearest Pneumati. In the present day, Virgil held Cornelius's soul too. Once the boy was gone, Ocharos laughed, like it was nothing. That was all that he ever did. He laughed at pain. He laughed at death. He thought it was entertaining to torture.

"I hate you!" Virgil screamed, before blasting Aegis toward Ocharos once again.

This time, it was larger, and the Aegis spell was able to actually cause Ocharos pain. Ocharos stepped back and growled, glancing at Virgil.

"You use this spell, yet you don't know the pain that it causes beings like us," Ocharos said.

"I don't care! You don't know the pain that you've caused!" Virgil yelled.

"Oh, I do. Now let me show you what it feels like to be burned by the 'light,'" Ocharos said.

Ocharos conjured a concentrated Aegis spell, and shot it toward Virgil. The spell hit him straight in the eye, burning like fire. Virgil screamed and stumbled backward into the Marrow Pit, to seal the fate of the Pneumati. Virgil's blood pooled at the top of the white liquid, like red and white marble. Ocharos only walked away during this with no care in the world, while Malachi followed.

During the panic, somehow Virgil was able to crawl out of the Marrow Pit. It hadn't taken full effect on him, but it did take some effects; his will was much stronger than Ocharos knew… The lively color had faded from his body, and the warmth of his blood was gone. His strength to fight kept him from becoming what he never wanted to be. Virgil's eye was useless now, and it bled while it burned. Without thinking, Virgil ran far away from that place with no care if he would ever return or not. He kept running and running until he couldn't run anymore, and then he lived by himself, wherever he could, until that day that the knights found him and brought him to Mountainglaive without question…

CHAPTER TWENTY NINE
We're Done Here

Everyone was back in the vestibule now, just as they were before. Virgil let go of Arael and stepped away to puke, like everyone else felt like doing. The legion masters were frozen, trying to comprehend how and what had just happened. Ariese sat down slowly and stared at the wall with his mouth open. Arael had tears in his eyes, while Orias was standing nearby with snot and tears running down his face.

Everyone had just seen all of that, and they all would rather have not seen it. Virgil wiped his mouth on his sleeve and looked up at Ariese. Unexpectedly, everyone else looked to the legion masters as well, except for Adonis and the legion of Geminiano. Virgil had earned their acceptance, and they were waiting for the legion masters to say something. They finally got a glimpse of what went on in Blightmire and what Virgil and the stolen kids had gone through all these years.

Ariese looked around, trying to think of something to say. "I- I told you that my decision was final, did I not?" He said.

Virgil nodded. "I understand and respect your decision..." He said, before turning around to walk away.

Everyone glared at Ariese and then Arael stepped forward. "Your decision doesn't matter," he told Ariese.

Virgil stopped when he heard Arael talk, and then waited for a reply from Ariese with his back turned.

"E- Excuse me?" Ariese asked.

"You heard me," Arael said.

Arael couldn't believe what he was doing. He felt empowered by speaking up, but he felt terrified too; his stomach felt like a tight knot. There was no way that he was going to let Ariese go on with this. It wasn't right. Next, Orias walked up and stopped next to Arael, and then Ego, and even Sir Enzo, Lady Agnes, Sir Gwenael and a few kids from the legions. Virgil turned around and couldn't believe what he was seeing.

Ariese glanced around dumbfounded. "Fine!" He said. "There will be no sentence for the Pneumati boy. He may stay... But we have our eyes on you..." He decided from the pressure.

Everyone nodded and then simply turned around to walk out of the room with Virgil, leaving the legion masters where they were. The Chancellor stood up and approached Ariese to speak with him. "I want you all out of my castle by sundown. My decision is final," she said, before walking out with everyone else.

CHAPTER THIRTY
Extorris

Months later... Arael, Ego, Orias and Virgil were all sitting outside, in the field behind the castle. There was no more training for them to do at Mountainglaive for now. They had found out that they were to be sent away for a while to complete their training as knights. They were all to be sent to separate places, so they were a bit sad about it. They were, however, able to clear Virgil of all the bad things that people had suddenly believed about him, and he was going to get to continue to be a knight of Mountainglaive with them.

Though they were to continue their paths as knights, they bore no symbols on their chests anymore. It was their choice to stray from the legion masters. They believed that in order to defeat evil, they had to stray from those who held it within their hearts. The other legions kept their crests, so the legion masters were never completely out of the picture... They still held their authority over Mountainglaive.

Orias was training Nerida to fly. She was big enough that she could do it now and the other three were cheering them on. They'd all become the best of friends, and they felt complete as a legion. They were more than friends, they were family.

"Try holding her up!" Ego said to Orias.

"I've done that before and she fell on her face," Orias said. "Besides, she's really heavy now."

It was true. Nerida was the size of a pygmy goat now. She acted like a goat too. Whenever she failed to fly, she'd get mad and make a goat noise before eating some dead grass. Orias watched the dragon eat grass in frustration, as he thought of some way that he could help her fly. "Nerida!" He said.

The dragon raised her head, with a mouth full of grass and looked to her rider.

"Try running!" Orias ran around in a circle while flapping his arms to show Nerida what he meant.

The dragon tilted her head to the side and leaped at Orias, before turning around and running away.

"Flap your wings!" Orias yelled.

"Flap, Nerida, flap!" Arael said.

Nerida flapped her wings clumsily and jumped up and down to try and get off of the ground with no luck.

"Fluttari Motis!" Virgil cast impatiently.

Suddenly, the dragon was launched off of the ground by the spell, but then she quickly caught herself and began gliding around! They all cheered for the dragon as she flew in circles all by herself. Nerida was happy too. She looked like she was smiling.

"Virgil, you launched the dragon," Arael laughed.

Virgil shrugged, "A little help never hurts…"

"You're a big cheater," Arael said.

"No, I'm impatient," Virgil said. "And it's not cheating!"

"Yes it is!"

"Fine… But I've never known better. I don't get how I could be cheating if it helps me get the upper hand."

"That's exactly what cheating is…" Arael said. "At least you've been nice to us with your cheating."

"Just keep thinking that and it'll be fine," Virgil laughed. "There's a lot that I still need to learn."

Arael laughed and pushed Virgil over, while they watched Nerida coming in for a landing. The dragon flew straight toward Orias at full speed, with no sign of slowing down. Orias's eyes widened in panic, and he started to run from her, but she was too fast and crashed into him, knocking him into a few summersaults across the ground. The others laughed as Orias came to a skidding stop, with the dragon on top of him.

"Are you okay?" Ego asked.

Orias pushed Nerida off and dusted the grass away from his pants before coming back to the group. "I'm fine…" He laughed. "I guess she needs more practice." Orias sat down with everyone else while he let Nerida roam around and eat more grass. "So?"

"So?" Ego repeated.

"I don't know…" Orias said.

Arael looked to Virgil and thought back on the day they all saw his past. He wondered who that boy with black hair really was to him. "Hey, Virgil. Can I ask who that boy with black hair was in your memories?" He asked. "I'm sorry he was killed."

"Well… It doesn't really matter anymore… I have a real family that I care about here now," Virgil answered. "Stuff happens…"

"Me too!" Orias said.

"Yeah… I could say the same," Ego added.

Arael nodded, "Me too… If I never get to see my dad again, then I could be alright."

"You'll see him again," Virgil said.

"If he's out there and he loves you and you love him, then you'll definitely see him again," Ego said.

They all smiled at each other and stared at the sky for a moment in silence, until Orias lied down in the crunchy, early spring grass. Next, they all slumped down and stared at the sky with him. The silence was nice, and it felt comfortable to just be there together.

"…Hey, guys?" Orias said. "If we're not under a legion master anymore, then what legion are we?" He asked.

"I never thought about that," Arael said.

"Well. We should come up with our own," Ego said. "What are we…? Misfits?"

"Weirdos is more like it," Arael said.

"Orias's Dragon People!" Orias said loudly.

"That's… Too long," Ego stated.

"You're right…" Orias said.

"Extorris?" Virgil asked.

"What does that mean? Is that a spell?" Orias asked.

"Part of one, but the word just stood out to me. It means outcast, exiled. Because we're different from everyone else," Virgil answered.

"Yeah! You're a Pneumati, Orias has a dragon and as far as I know, Arael is the only Dreamwalker in the entire castle! And I'm the best Protector in the land!" Ego said. "I think I like it. It has a ring to it, like a good band name."

"I guess it's decided then? The legion of Extorris. Sounds like we can kick some butt," Arael said.

"Now all we need is a symbol!" Orias said.

"Leave that to me!" Arael said.

Arael put his fist into the air and then everybody else did the same. "We will from now on be known as the legion of Extorris. The best legion that there ever was! We won't ever break apart, and we won't ever be defeated! We will destroy all evil in our path!" He said. "Extorris!"

"Extorris!" Everyone else repeated, boldly jutting their fists into the air.

Arael's journal was lying in the grass nearby, left open on the very last page; the last sketch that he could fit into it. It was the most detailed sketch in the journal; a sketch of him and his new family, all together.

THE BEGINNING

Acknowledgements

I want to give a huge thanks to my mom, who always supports me and helps me when I write. She helped me go through this book so many times and make sure it was the best as we could make it be on our own. Without her, my work would be nothing and so would I. I love her with all of my heart.

Thank you, beta readers, my mom, and my grandma, who gave be some good feedback to help me see the book through fresh eyes. Connor especially, who gave extremely good feedback, and gave me notes to help to improve certain aspects of my writing.

Thank you, my friends and family for encouraging me to pursue my dreams rather than turning me away, and for their support in everything that I do, and everything that I am.

Special thanks to Josh, Nathan, Jim, and my brother Ronan, who helped me with their great support, even when I didn't support myself.

This book is dedicated to my dad, because of his love for the fantasy genre, which inspired me to write the story of Extorris.

About The Author

Raphael "Raph" was born to write books, literally. He started writing novels, comics, and doing his own artwork at the age of 8 years old. Now Raph is a 17 year old introverted genius that likes chocolate, his dogs, and Marvel comics. Raph graduated from Homeschool in 2017 and shortly after finished his first full book Extorris. He is currently working on the follow up books to this series, so watch for that.

You can follow Raph's journey on Facebook, under Rapheal Lucchesi which will have some cool artwork from the book, and exciting information about upcoming books as well. Raph is a big supporter of the LGBTQ+ community, and hopes that anyone who reads his books will find a little bit of themselves in the characters.

Everything starts out as only a simple idea, but it will blossom into something great with enough love and hard work. If you love what you do, and you never give up, then good things will come to you. It may not seem like it, but everything happens for a reason. Your dream will happen when it is meant to happen, but only if you make it possible.

Made in the USA
San Bernardino, CA
03 July 2017